To Be a Man

Also by Nicole Krauss

Man Walks Into a Room

The History of Love

Great House

Forest Dark

To Be a Man

Stories

Nicole Krauss

HARPER

An Imprint of HarperCollinsPublishers

TO BE A MAN. Copyright © 2020 by Nicole Krauss. All rights reserved. Printed in the United States of America. No part of this book may be used or reproduced in any manner whatsoever without written permission except in the case of brief quotations embodied in critical articles and reviews. For information in the United States, address HarperCollins Publishers, 195 Broadway, New York, NY 10007, USA. In Canada, address HarperCollins Publishers Ltd, Bay Adelaide Centre, East Tower, 22 Adelaide Street West, 41st Floor, Toronto, Ontario, M5H 4E3, Canada.

HarperCollins books may be purchased for educational, business, or sales promotional use. For information, please email the Special Markets Department in the United States at SPsales@harpercollins.com or in Canada at HCOrder @harpercollins.com.

FIRST EDITION

Designed by Leah Carlson-Stanisic

Library of Congress Cataloging-in-Publication Data has been applied for.

Library and Archives Canada Cataloguing in Publication information is available upon request.

ISBN 978-0-06-243102-8
ISBN 978-1-4434-4940-3 (Canada hc)
ISBN 978-1-4434-4941-0 (Canada pbk)

20 21 22 23 24   LSC   10 9 8 7 6 5 4 3 2 1

For Sasha and Cy

Contents

To Be a Man

Switzerland

It's been thirty years since I saw Soraya. In that time I tried to find her only once. I think I was afraid of seeing her, afraid of trying to understand her now that I was older and maybe could, which I suppose is the same as saying that I was afraid of myself: of what I might discover beneath my understanding. The years passed and I thought of her less and less. I went to university, then graduate school, got married sooner than I imagined and had two daughters only a year apart. If Soraya came to mind at all, flickering past in a mercurial chain of associations, she would recede again just as quickly.

I met Soraya when I was thirteen, the year that my family spent abroad in Switzerland. "Expect the worst" might have been the family motto, had my father not explicitly instructed us that it was "Trust no one, suspect everyone." We lived on the edge of a cliff, though our house was impressive. We were European

Jews, even in America, which is to say that catastrophic things had happened, and might happen again. Our parents fought violently, their marriage forever on the verge of collapse. Financial ruin also loomed; we were warned that the house would soon have to be sold. No money had come in since our father left the family business after years of daily screaming battles with our grandfather. When our father went back to school, I was two, my brother four. Premed courses were followed by medical school at Columbia, then a residency in orthopedic surgery at the Hospital for Special Surgery, though what kind of special we didn't know. During those eleven years of training, my father logged countless nights on call in the emergency room, greeting a grisly parade of victims: car crashes, motorcycle accidents, and once the crash of an Avianca airplane headed for Bogotá that nosedived into a hill in Cove Neck. At bottom, he might have clung to the superstitious belief that his nightly confrontations with horror could save his family from it. But on a stormy September afternoon in my father's final year of residency, my grandmother was hit by a speeding van on the corner of First Avenue and Fiftieth Street, causing hemorrhaging in her brain. When my father got to Bellevue Hospital, his mother was lying on a stretcher in the emergency room. She squeezed his hand and slipped into a coma. Six weeks later, she died. Less than a year after her death, my father finished his residency and moved our family to Switzerland, where he began a fellowship in trauma.

That Switzerland—neutral, alpine, orderly—has the best institute for trauma in the world seems paradoxical. The whole country had, back then, the atmosphere of a sanatorium or asylum. Instead of padded walls it had the snow, which muffled and softened everything, until after so many centuries the Swiss just went about instinctively muffling themselves. Or that was the point: a country singularly obsessed with controlled reserve and conformity, with engineering watches, with the promptness of trains, would, it follows, have an advantage in the emergency of a body smashed to pieces. That Switzerland is also a country of many languages is what granted my brother and me unexpected reprieve from the familial gloom. The institute was in Basel, where the language is Schweizerdeutsch, but my mother was of the opinion that we should continue our French. Schweizerdeutsch was only a hairbreadth removed from Deutsch, and we were not allowed to touch anything even remotely Deutsch, the language of our maternal grandmother, whose entire family had been murdered by the Nazis. We were therefore enrolled in the École Internationale in Geneva. My brother lived in the boardinghouse on campus, but as I'd just turned thirteen, I didn't make the cutoff. To save me from the traumas associated with Deutsch, a solution was found for me in the western outskirts of Geneva, and in September 1987 I became a boarder in the home of a substitute English teacher named Mrs. Elderfield. She had hair dyed the color of straw, and the rosy cheeks of someone raised in a damp climate, but she seemed old all the same.

My small bedroom had a window that looked onto an apple tree. On the day that I arrived, red apples were fallen all around it, rotting in the autumn sun. Inside the room was a small desk, a reading chair, and a bed at whose foot was folded a gray wool army blanket old enough to have been used in a world war. The brown carpet was worn down to the weave at the threshold.

Two other boarders, both eighteen, shared the back bedroom at the end of the hall. All three of our narrow beds had once belonged to Mrs. Elderfield's sons, but they had grown up and moved away long before we girls arrived to occupy them. There were no photographs of her boys, so we never knew what they looked like, but we rarely forgot that they had once slept in our beds. Between Mrs. Elderfield's absent sons and us there was a carnal link. There was also no mention of Mrs. Elderfield's husband, if she'd ever had one. She was not the sort of person who invited personal questions. When it was time to sleep, she switched off our lights without a word.

On my first evening in the house, I sat on the floor of the older girls' room among their piles of clothes. Back home, the girls sprayed themselves with a cheap men's cologne called Drakar. But the strong perfume that permeated these girls' clothes was unfamiliar to me. Mixed with their body heat and the chemistry of their skin, it mellowed, but from time to time it built up so strongly in their bedsheets and tossed-off shirts and bags that Mrs. Elderfield forced open the windows, and the cold air once again stripped everything bare.

I listened as the older girls discussed their lives in coded words I didn't understand. They laughed at my naïveté, but they were both only ever kind to me. Marie had come from Bangkok via Boston, and Soraya from the sixteenth arrondissement of Paris via Tehran, where her father had been the royal engineer to the shah before the revolution had sent their family into exile, too late to pack Soraya's toys but in time to transfer most of their liquid assets. Wildness—sex, stimulants, a refusal to comply—is what had landed them both in Switzerland for an extra year of school, a thirteenth year that previously neither of them had ever heard of.

WE USED TO set out for school in the dark. To get to the bus stop, we had to cross a field, which by November was covered in snow that the sheared brown stalks sworded through. We were always late. I was always the only one who'd eaten. Someone's hair was always wet, the ends frozen. We huddled under the enclosure, inhaling secondhand smoke from Soraya's cigarette. The bus took us past the Armenian church to the orange tram. Then it was a long ride to the school on the other side of the city. Because of our different schedules we rode back alone. Only on the first day, at Mrs. Elderfield's insistence, did Marie and I meet up to travel together, but we took the tram in the wrong direction and ended up in France. After that I learned the way, and usually I broke up the journey by stopping in the tobacco shop next to the tram stop, where before catching the bus I bought myself some candy from the open containers that, according to my mother, were crawling with strangers' germs.

I'd never been so happy or so free. It wasn't only the difficult and anxious atmosphere of our family that I'd gotten away from but also my miserable school back home, with its petty, hormonal girls, olympic in their cruelty. I was too young for a driver's license, so there was never any means of escape except through books or walking in the woods behind our house. Now I spent the hours after school wandering the city of Geneva. I never had any destination, though I often ended up by the lake, where

I watched the tourist cruises come and go, or invented stories about the people I saw, especially the ones who came to make out on the benches. Sometimes I tried on clothes at H&M, or wandered around the Old City, where I was drawn back to the imposing monument to the Reformation, to the inscrutable faces of towering stone Protestants of whose names I can only recall John Calvin's. I hadn't yet heard of Borges, and yet at no other time in my life was I closer to the Argentine writer who had died in Geneva the year before, and who, in a letter explaining his wish to be buried in his adopted city, wrote that there he had always felt "mysteriously happy." Years later, a friend gave me Borges's *Atlas*, and I was startled to see a huge photo of those somber giants I used to visit regularly, anti-Semites all, who believed in predestination and the absolute sovereignty of God. In it John Calvin leans slightly forward to gaze down at the blind Borges, seated on the stone ledge holding his cane, chin tilted upward. Between John Calvin and Borges, the photo seemed to say, there was a great attunement. There was no attunement between John Calvin and me, but I too had sat on that same ledge looking up at him.

Sometimes in my wanderings a man would stare at me without letting up, or come on to me in French. These brief encounters embarrassed me, and left me with a feeling of shame. Often the men were African, with sparkling white smiles, but one time, as I stood looking into the window of a chocolate shop, a European man in a beautiful suit came up behind me. He leaned in, his face touching my hair, and in faintly accented English, whispered, "I could break you in two with one hand." Then he continued on his way, very calmly, as if he were a boat sailing on still water. I ran all the way to the tram stop, where I stood gasping for breath until the tram arrived and squeaked mercifully to a stop, and then slumped into a seat behind the driver.

We were expected at the dinner table at 6:30 sharp. The wall behind Mrs. Elderfield's seat was hung with small oil paintings of alpine scenes, and even now an image of a chalet, or cows with bells, or some Heidi gathering berries in her checked apron brings back the aroma of fish and boiled potatoes. Very little was said during those dinners. Or maybe it only seems so in comparison to how much was said in the back bedroom.

Marie's father met her mother in Bangkok while he was a GI, and had brought her back to America, where he set her up with a Cadillac Seville and a ranch house in Silver Spring, Maryland. When they divorced, her mother went back to Thailand, and for the next fifteen years Marie was tossed and tugged between them. In the last few years she had lived exclusively with her mother in Bangkok, where she had a boyfriend with whom she was madly, jealously in love, and would stay out with him all night dancing in clubs, drunk or high. When Marie's mother, at her wit's end and busy with her own boyfriend, told her father about the situation, he yanked her out of Thailand and deposited her in Switzerland, known for its "finishing" schools that polished the wild and the dark out of girls and contained them into well-mannered women. Ecolint was not such a school, but Marie, it turned out, was already too old for a proper finishing school. She was, in the estimation of these schools, already finished. And not in the good way. And so instead Marie was sent to do an extra year of high school at Ecolint, which went to the thirteenth grade. Along with Mrs. Elderfield's house rules, there were strict instructions from Marie's father about her curfew, and after Marie got into Mrs. Elderfield's cooking wine, these stringent regulations were tightened even further. Because of this, on the weekends that I did not take the train to Basel to see my parents, Marie and I were often home together while Soraya was out.

Unlike Marie, Soraya didn't radiate trouble. At least not the sort of trouble that comes of recklessness, of a desire to cross whatever boundaries or limits others set for one without consideration of the consequences. If anything, Soraya radiated a sense of authority, exquisite for the fact that it derived from an inner source. Her outward appearance was neat and composed. She was small, no taller than I was, and wore her dark straight hair cut in what she called a Chanel bob, made up her eyes with winged eyeliner, and had a downy mustache that she made no effort to conceal, because she must have known that it added to her allure. But she always spoke in a low voice, as if she only trafficked in secrets, a habit that might have been formed during her childhood in revolutionary Iran, or in her adolescence, when her appetite for boys, and then men, quickly outgrew what was considered acceptable by her family. On Sundays, when none of us had much to do, the three of us would spend the day closed up in the back bedroom listening to cassettes and, in that low-slung voice further deepened by smoking, descriptions of the men Soraya had been with and the things she'd done with them. If these accounts never shocked me, it was partly because I didn't yet have a solid enough sense of sex, let alone the erotic, to really know what to expect from it. But it was also because of the coolness with which Soraya told her stories. She had about her a kind of unassailability. And yet I suppose she felt the need to test whatever it was at her core, like all natural gifts that come to us before effort, and what might happen if it failed her. The sex she described seemed to have little to do with pleasure. On the contrary, it was as if she were submitting herself to a trial. Only when, woven into Soraya's discursive stories, Tehran came up and she recounted her memories of that city was her sense of pleasure truly palpable.

NOVEMBER, AFTER THE arrival of the snow: it must have been November already when the businessman showed up in our conversations. Dutch, more than twice Soraya's age, he lived in a house with no curtains on an Amsterdam canal, but every couple of weeks he came to Geneva on business. A banker, as I recall. The lack of curtains I remember because he told Soraya that he only fucked his wife with the lights on when he was sure people across the Herengracht could see her. He stayed at the Hôtel Royal, and it was in the restaurant of that hotel, where her uncle had taken her for tea, that Soraya first met him. He was sitting a few tables away, and while her uncle droned on in Farsi about all of the money his children spent, Soraya watched the banker delicately debone his fish. Wielding his utensils with precision, a look of absolute calm on his face, the man extracted the skeleton whole. Not once as he proceeded to devour the fish did he stop to remove a small bone from his mouth, as everyone does. He performed the operation with perfection, slowly, without any sign of hunger. Then he ate his fish without choking, without even making the passing grimace that comes with the displeasure of being speared in the throat by a tiny, errant bone. It's a certain kind of man that can take what is essentially an act of violence and turn it into elegance. While her uncle was in the men's room, the man called for his check, paid in cash, and rose to leave, buttoning his sports jacket. But instead of going straight out the doors that led to the lobby, he detoured past Soraya's table, on which he dropped a five-hundred-franc note. His room number was written in blue ink next to Albrecht von Haller's face, as if it were Albrecht von Haller who was affording her this bit of precious information. Later, while she was kneeling on the hotel bed, freezing in the cold gusting in through the open terrace doors, the banker told her that he always got a room with a view overlooking the lake because the powerful stream of its fountain, which shot up hundreds of feet into the air, aroused him. As she repeated this to us, lying flat on the floor with her feet up on the twin bed of Mrs. Elderfield's son, she laughed and couldn't stop. And yet, despite the laughter, an arrangement had been made. From then on, if he wished to let Soraya know of his impending arrival, the banker would call the phone at Mrs. Elderfield's house and pretend to be her uncle. The five-hundred-franc note Soraya put away in the drawer of her night table.

AT THE TIME, Soraya was seeing other men. There was the boy her age, the son of a diplomat who came to pick her up in his father's sports car, the transmission of which he destroyed on their ride to Montreux. And there was an Algerian in his early twenties who worked as a waiter in a restaurant near the school. She slept with the son of the diplomat, whereas the Algerian, who was genuinely in love with her, she only allowed to kiss her. Because he had grown up poor like Camus, she projected on him a fantasy. But when he had nothing to say about the sun he was raised under, she began to lose feeling for him. It sounds cold, but later I experienced it in myself: the sudden disassociation that comes with the fear of realizing how intimate one has been with one who is not at all what you imagined, but something other, entirely unknown. So when the banker demanded that Soraya drop both the diplomat's son and the Algerian, it was not difficult for Soraya to comply. It excused her of responsibility for the Algerian's pain.

On the morning before we left for school, the telephone rang. When she cut things off with each of these lovers, the banker instructed, she was to wear a skirt with nothing underneath. She told us this as we crossed the frozen field on our way to the bus stop, and we laughed. But then Soraya stopped and cupped her lighter from the wind. In the brightness of the flame I caught her eyes, and for the first time I felt afraid for her. Or afraid of her, maybe. Afraid of what she lacked, or what she possessed, that drove her beyond the place where others would draw the limit.

SORAYA HAD TO call the banker from the pay phone at school at certain times of the day, even when it meant excusing herself in the middle of class. When she arrived at the Hôtel Royal for one of their meetings, an envelope would be waiting for her at the front desk, containing elaborate instructions for what she was to do when she entered the room. I don't know what happened if she failed to follow the banker's rules, or follow them to his exacting standards. It didn't occur to me that she might have allowed herself to be punished. Barely out of childhood, I think what I understood then, however simply, was that she was engaged in a game. A game that at any moment she could have refused to go on playing. That she, of all people, knew how easily rules could be broken, but that she elected, in this instance alone, to follow them—what could I have understood then about that? I don't know. Just as thirty years later I don't know if what I saw in her eyes when the flame illuminated them was perversity, or recklessness, or fear, or its opposite: the unyielding nature of her will.

DURING THE CHRISTMAS break Marie flew to Boston, I went to stay with my family in Basel, and Soraya went home to Paris. When we returned two weeks later, something had changed in her. She seemed withdrawn, closed up in herself, and spent her time listening to her Walkman in bed, reading books in French, or smoking out the window. Whenever the phone rang, she jumped up to answer it, and when it was for her she shut the door and sometimes didn't come out for hours. Marie came to my room more and more often, because, she said, being around Soraya gave her the creeps. As we lay together in my narrow bed, Marie would tell me stories about Bangkok, and however full of drama they were, Marie could still laugh at herself and make me laugh. Looking back, I think that she taught me something that, however many times I have forgotten it and remembered it since then, has never really left me: something about the absurdity, and also the truth, of the dramas we need to feel fully alive.

From January, then, until April, what I mostly remember are the things that were happening to me. Kate, the American girl I became close with, who was the oldest of four sisters, and lived in a large house in the neighborhood of Champel, and showed me her father's collection of *Playboy* magazines. The small daughter of Mrs. Elderfield's neighbor whom I sometimes babysat, and who one night sat up in bed screaming when she saw a praying mantis on the wall, lit by the headlights of a car. My long walks after school. The weekends in Basel, where I would entertain my little sister with games in the kitchen to distract her from my parents' arguments. And Shareef, a boy in my class with an easy smile whom I walked to the lake with one afternoon, and made out with on a bench. It was the first time I'd kissed a boy, and when he pushed his tongue into my mouth, the feeling it ignited was both tender and violent. I dug my nails into his back, and he kissed me harder, we writhed together on the bench like the couples I'd sometimes watched from afar. On the tram ride home I could smell him on my skin, and a feeling of horror took hold of me at the thought of having to see him again in school the next day. When I did, I looked past him as if he didn't exist, but with my gaze softly focused, so that I could still see the blur of his hurt in the corner of my eye.

Of that time, I remember, too, how once I came home from school and found Soraya in the bathroom, doing her makeup in front of the mirror. Her eyes were shining, and she seemed happy and light again, as she hadn't been for weeks. She called me in, and wanted to brush and braid my hair. Her cassette player was balanced on the edge of the bathtub, and while her fingers worked through my hair, she sang along. And then, when she turned to reach for a hairpin behind her, I saw the purple bruise on her throat.

And yet I never really doubted her strength. Never doubted that she was in control and doing what she wanted. Playing a game according to rules she had agreed to, if not invented. Only looking back do I realize how much I wanted to see her that way: strong-willed and free, invulnerable and under her own command. From my walks alone in Geneva, I already understood that the power to attract men, when it comes, arrives with a terrifying vulnerability. But I wanted to believe that the balance of power could be tipped in one's favor by strength or fearlessness or something I couldn't name. Soon after things began with the banker, Soraya had told us that once his wife called on the hotel phone, and he'd instructed Soraya to go into the bathroom, but she'd refused and instead lay listening on the bed. The naked banker turned his back but had no choice but to go on talking to his wife, whose call he hadn't expected. He spoke to her in Dutch, Soraya said, but in the same tone the men in her own family spoke to their mothers: gravely, with a touch of fear. And as she listened, she knew something had been exposed that he had not wished to expose, and which shifted the balance between them. I preferred that story, if I preferred any story at all, to trying to understand the bruise on Soraya's neck.

IT WAS THE first week of May when she didn't return home. Mrs. Elderfield woke us at dawn, demanding we tell her whatever we knew about Soraya's whereabouts. Marie shrugged and looked at her chipped nail polish, and I tried to follow her cue until Mrs. Elderfield said that she was going to call both Soraya's parents and the police, and that if something had happened to her, if she were in danger and we were withholding any information, we wouldn't be forgiven or be able to forgive ourselves. Marie looked scared, and, seeing her face, I began to cry. A few hours later, the police arrived. Alone with the detective and his partner in the kitchen, I told them everything I knew, which I realized as I spoke—losing the thread, confusing myself—was not so much. After they interrogated Marie, they went to the back bedroom and combed through Soraya's things. Afterward it looked as if the bedroom had been ransacked: everything, even her underwear, strewn across the floor and bed with an air of violation.

That night, the second Soraya was missing, there was a huge storm. Marie and I lay awake in my bed, neither one of us speaking of the things we feared. In the morning, the crunch of gravel under the wheels of a car woke us, and we jumped out of bed to look out the window. But when the door of the taxi opened, it was a man who emerged, his lips drawn tight below his heavy black mustache. In the familiar features of her father, some truth about Soraya's origins was revealed, exposing the illusion of her autonomy.

Mrs. Elderfield made us repeat to Mr. Sassani the things we'd already told the police. He was a tall and intimidating man, his face drawn into a knot of anger, and I think she wasn't brave enough to do it herself. In the end, Marie—emboldened by her new authority and the sensational quality of the news she had to deliver—did most of the talking. Mr. Sassani listened in silence, and it was impossible to say whether what he felt was fear or fury. Both, it must have been. He turned toward the door. He wanted to go immediately to the Hôtel Royal. Mrs. Elderfield tried to calm him. She repeated what was already known: that the banker had checked out two days before, the room had been searched, nothing had been turned up. The police were doing everything they could. The banker had rented a car that they were working to track down. The only thing to do was to stay here and wait until there was some news.

In the hours that followed, Mr. Sassani paced grimly in front of the windows of the living room. As the royal engineer to the shah, he must have ensured against all kinds of collapse. But then the shah himself had fallen, and the vast and intricate structure of Mr. Sassani's life had crumbled beneath his feet, making a mockery of the physics of safety. He'd sent his oldest daughter to Switzerland because of its promise to restore order and safety, but even Switzerland hadn't kept Soraya safe, and this betrayal seemed too much for him. At any moment, it seemed he might shout or cry out.

IN THE END, Soraya came home on her own. On her own— just as she had gotten into it on her own, of her own choosing. Crossing the newly green field that evening, arriving at the door disheveled but whole. Her eyes were bloodshot and the makeup around them was smeared, but she was calm. She didn't even express surprise at the sight of her father, only winced when he shouted her name, the last syllable muffled by a gasp or sob. He lunged for her, and for a moment it seemed that he was going to yell or raise his hand to her, but she didn't flinch, and instead he pulled her to him and embraced her, his eyes filled with tears. He spoke to her urgently, angrily, in Farsi, but she said little back. She was tired, she said in English, she needed to sleep. In a voice unnaturally high, Mrs. Elderfield asked if she wanted anything to eat. Soraya shook her head, as if there was nothing anymore that any of us could offer that she needed, and turned toward the long corridor that led to the back bedroom. As she passed me, she stopped, reached out her hand, and touched my hair. And then, very slowly, she continued on her way.

The next day her father took her back to Paris. I don't remember if we said goodbye. I think we thought, Marie and I, that she would come back, that she would return to finish the school year and tell us everything. But she never came back. She left it to us to decide for ourselves what had happened to her, and in my mind I saw her in that moment when she'd touched my hair with a sad smile, and believed that what I'd seen had been a kind of grace: the grace that comes of having pushed oneself to the brink, of having confronted some darkness or fear and won. At the end of June, my father finished his fellowship and, expert in trauma, moved us back to New York. The mean girls took an interest in me when I returned to school in September, and wanted to befriend me. At a party, one of them turned a circle around me while I stood calmly, very still. She marveled at how I'd changed, and at my clothes bought abroad. I had gone out into the world and come back, and though I wasn't saying anything, they sensed that I knew things. For a while Marie sent me cassettes on which she'd recorded herself talking to me, telling me all the things that were happening in her life. But eventually they stopped arriving, and we lost touch too. And that was the end of Switzerland for me.

In my mind, that was also the end of Soraya: as I said, I never

saw her again, and tried to look for her only once, the summer
when I was nineteen and living in Paris. Even then, I barely
tried—calling two Sassani families who were listed in the phone
book and then giving up. And yet if it hadn't been for her, I don't
know that I would have gotten on the motorcycle of the young
man who washed dishes at the restaurant across the street from
my apartment on the rue de Chevreuse, and ridden back with
him to his apartment in the outskirts of the city, or gone to a
bar with the older man who lived on the floor below me, who
went on about the job I knew he would never get for me at the
nightclub he managed, and then, when we got back to the building, lunged at me on the landing in front of his door, tackling
me in an embrace. I watched a movie on the dishwasher's sofa,
and afterward he told me it was dangerous to go home with men
I didn't know, and drove me back to my apartment in silence.
And somehow I broke free of the nightclub manager and ran up
another floor to the safety of my own apartment, though for
the rest of the summer I was terrified of passing him on the
stairs, and listened for his comings and goings before I worked
up the courage to open my door and bolt down the stairs. I told
myself that I did these things because I was in Paris to practice my French, and had resolved to speak to anyone who would
speak to me. But all summer I was aware that Soraya might have
been near, somewhere in that city, that I was close to her and
close to something in myself that drew me and frightened me a
little, as she did. She had gone further than anyone I knew in a
game that was never only a game, one that was about power and
fear, about the refusal to comply with the vulnerabilities one is
born into.

But I myself wasn't able to go very far with it. I think I didn't have the courage, and after that summer I was never again so bold or so reckless. I had one boyfriend after another, all of them gentle and a little afraid of me, and then I got married and had two daughters of my own. The oldest has my husband's sandy hair; if she were walking in a field in autumn, you could lose her easily. But the younger one stands out wherever she is. She grows and develops in contrast with everything around her. It's wrong, dangerous even, to imagine that a person has any choice in her looks. And yet I'd swear that my daughter had something to do with the black hair and green eyes that always attract attention, even when she's standing in a chorus of other children. She's only twelve, and still small, but already men look at her when she walks in the street or rides the subway. And she doesn't hunch, or put up her hood, or hide away behind her headphones the way her friends do. She stands erect and still like a queen, which only makes her even more of an object of their fascination. She has a proudness about her that refuses to grow small, but if it was only that, I might not have begun to fear for her. It's her curiosity in her own power, its reach and its limit, that frightens me. Though maybe the truth is that when I am not afraid for her, I envy her. One day I saw it: how she looked back at the man in the business suit who stood across the subway car from her, burning a hole through her with his eyes. Her stare was a challenge. If a friend had been riding with her, she might have turned her face slowly to her, without taking her eyes off the man, and said something to invoke laughter. It was then that Soraya came back to me, and since then I have been what I can only call haunted by her. By her, and how a person can happen to you and only half a lifetime later does this happening ripen, burst, and deliver itself. Soraya with her downy mustache and her winged eyeliner and her laugh, that deep laugh that came from her stomach, when she told us about the Dutch banker's arousal. He could have broken her in two with one hand, but either she was already broken, or she wasn't going to break.

Zusya on the Roof

Heels dug into the tar paper, twenty-three floors above 110th Street, cradling his newborn grandson—how did he wind up here? It was not a simple thing, as his father would say. Simplicity was not his patrimony.

To begin specifically: Brodman had been dead for two weeks, but then, sadly, he had come back to this world, where he'd spent fifty years trying to write unnecessary books. There had been complications after surgery for a tumor in his bowel. Hooked to a respirator, bags for every fluid going in or coming out, for fifteen days his body lay on a gurney, fighting a medieval war against double pneumonia. For two weeks Brodman hung in the balance, dead and not dead. Like the house in Leviticus, he had been infested with plague: they scraped him clean and took him apart, stone by stone. Either it would work or it wouldn't. Either the plague would be gone or it had already spread through him.

While waiting for the verdict, he dreamed wildly. Such hallucinations! Drugged, his temperature soaring, he dreamed he was the anti-Herzl, lecturing from coast to coast to crowds so huge they watched simulcasts of the simulcasts. A West Bank rabbi issued a fatwa on his head, with a ten-million-dollar bounty funded by a Jewish casino king. Hunted for treason, Brodman was hidden in a safe house somewhere in the heart of Germany. Outside his window, he could see the rolling hills of—Bavaria? Weserbergland? He was spared the details for his own good, in case he should break down and place a phone call to his wife, Mira, or his lawyer, or Rabbi Chanan Ben-Zvi of Gush Etzion. And if he did call the rabbi, what would he say? *I surrender, come and get me, third dirt road on the left, past the dairy farm where Brunhilde is singing "Edelweiss" at the udders, and don't forget your assault rifle*? Or maybe the rabbi planned to slit Brodman's throat with a carving knife.

From the German safe house, he held counsel with Buber, Rabbi Akiva, and Gershom Scholem, who relaxed on a bearskin rug, scratching behind its ears. He sat with Maimonides in the back of a bulletproof car; there was no end to the talking. He saw Moses ibn Ezra and heard Salo Baron, to whom he called, waving his arms to disperse the smoke. He couldn't see him, but knew he was in that swirling nebula, breathing heavily— Salo Wittmayer Baron, who knew twenty languages and had testified at Eichmann's trial, the first man to receive a chair in Jewish history at a university in the Western world. *Salo, what have you brought on us?*

Enormous things happened to him during those feverish weeks, unspeakable revelations. Unbuttoned from time, transient and transcendental, Brodman saw the true shape of his life, how it had torqued always in the direction of duty. Not only his life but the life of his people—the three thousand years of treacherous remembering, highly regarded suffering, and waiting.

On the fifteenth day, his fever broke and he woke to find himself cured. His body was habitable; he would live a little more. All that remained, according to the passage in Leviticus, was the ritual atonement that called for two birds, one to be sacrificed and the other left to live. One killed, the other dipped in the blood of its kin, shaken seven times around the house, then set free. Such reprieve! He never read the passage without crying. *But he shall let go the living bird out of the city into the open fields, and make atonement for the house: and it shall be clean.*

While he was hallucinating, his only grandchild arrived into the world. In his weakened state, Brodman half believed that his own mental work had performed the labor. His younger daughter, Ruthie, didn't like men. When she'd announced that she was pregnant at forty-one, Brodman had accepted it as a miracle of immaculate conception. But the happiness was short-lived. A few months later, he'd gone in for a routine blood test, which led to a colonoscopy, which led, a month and a half before the child was due, to the discovery of his own gestation. If he believed in such things, he might have taken it for something mystical. Sweating and moaning, in horrific pain from his gut, he had pushed the idea of the child through the tight passage of incredulity and borne him into existence. It had almost killed him.

No, it *had* killed him. He had died for the child, and then, by some miracle, he had been brought back again. For what?

They removed the respirator early one morning. The young doctor stood over him, eyes moist from the miracle he'd performed. Brodman inhaled his first breath of real air in two weeks, and it went to his head. Dizzy, he pulled the doctor close, so close that all he could see was his teeth, so white, so blindingly beautiful, and to those teeth, which were the closest thing in the room to God, he whispered, "I wasn't Zusya." The doctor didn't understand. He had to say it again, pushing the words hard out of his mouth. Finally, he was heard. "Of course not," the doctor said soothingly, freeing himself from his patient's weak grip and gently patting the hand speared through with the IV tube. "You were Professor Brodman, and you're still him."

If they hadn't cut his stomach muscles, he might have laughed. What could such a person know of regret? Probably he didn't have children yet. By the look of him, not even a wife. Everything was before him. Soon he'd go for his coffee, filled with the promise of the day. And just that morning, he'd brought a dead man back to life! What could he know of a life misspent? Yes, Brodman had been Brodman and was still Brodman, and yet he had failed to be Brodman, just as Rabbi Zusya had failed to be the man he should have been. He had learned the tale as a boy: how after the rebbe from Hanipol died, he stood awaiting God's judgment, ashamed that he had not been Moses or Abraham. But when God appeared at last, He asked only, "Why weren't you Zusya?" The story ended there, but Brodman had dreamed the rest: how God concealed Himself again, and Zusya, all alone, whispered, "Because I was a Jew, and there was no room left to be anything else, not even Zusya."

The washed morning light filed through the hospital window, and a pigeon flapped loose from the sill. The glass was frosted to hide the brick wall across the way, and what he could see of the bird was only a changing form moving upward. But he heard the scramble of wings in his thoughts as a kind of punctuation, like a comma striking the white page. It had been years since his mind was so clear or focused. Death had scoured it of the extraneous. His thoughts were of a different quality now, and bore sharply through. He had the feeling that at last he had got to the bottom of everything. He wanted to tell Mira. But where was Mira? All through the long days of illness she had sat in a chair at his bedside, leaving only for a few hours each night to sleep. In that instant, Brodman understood that his grandson had been born while he was dead. He wanted to know: Had they named the boy after him?

He'd retired from teaching years ago, and was said to be writing the masterwork that would synthesize a lifetime of scholarship. But no one had seen the pages, and rumors circulated around the department at Columbia. As far back as he could remember, he had known the answers—his life had floated on a great ocean of understanding, and he'd had only to dip his cup. He had not noticed the slow evaporation of that ocean until it was too late. He had ceased to understand. He had not understood for years. Every day he sat at his desk in the cramped back room of the apartment filled with tribal art that he and Mira had bought cheaply forty years ago on a trip to New Mexico.

For years he'd sat, but nothing had come. He'd even thought of writing his memoirs, but got only as far as filling a notebook with the names of people he'd once known. When his old students came by, he sat under the primitive masks and held forth on the predicament of the Jewish historian. The Jews had finished writing history long ago, he said. When the rabbis closed the canon of the Bible, it was because they felt they had more than enough history. Two thousand years ago the door was shut on sacred history, the only kind a Jew had any use for. Then came the zealotry and the messianism, the savagery of the Romans, the river of blood, the fire, the destruction, and, finally, exile. From then on, the Jews decided to live outside history. History was what happened to other people while the Jews were waiting for the Messiah to come. In the meantime the rabbis busied themselves with Jewish memory only, and for two millennia that memory had sustained an entire people. So who was he—who were any of them—to rock the boat?

Having heard it all before, his students came by less and less. Ruthie could bear to stay for only fifteen minutes. His older daughter had long ago been lost to him. Occasionally, she took a break from throwing herself in front of Israeli bulldozers in the West Bank to call home. But if he picked up, instead of Mira, she hung up and went back to the Palestinians. For a moment, he would hear her breathing. "Carol?" But he was answered by the dial tone. What had he ever done to her? He had not been a good father. But had he been so terrible? Absorbed in his academic life, he had left the girls in Mira's hands. Had there been something beneath that choice? What interest they might have had in him waned. At night, when Mira braided their coppery hair before bed, the delicate lacework of their days had come spooling out, the triumphs and the disappointments. He was neither expected nor wanted during this ritual, so he kept to himself in the back room, converted into a study after Carol was born. But the sense of being shut out, powerless and irrelevant, stoked his fury. Later, he always regretted the things he said.

And yet his daughters hadn't been cowed by him. They had done what they wanted to do. His own children had not suffered under the same filial yoke as he. An only child, Brodman had no more been able to betray his parents than kick them in the face. Their lives had rested on his back like a house of cards. His father had arrived at Ellis Island as a scholar of ancient languages, and come out the other end as a Hebrew teacher. His mother had become a housecleaner for well-to-do Jews in the Bronx. When Brodman was born, she'd stopped working, but in her mind she went on navigating rooms, staircases, corners, and corridors. In his early years, she would get lost traversing those spaces. Can a child understand that his mother is losing herself? Brodman had not understood. After she was taken away, he was alone with his father. With grim piety and meticulousness, his father had schooled him in what was expected. Every day at dawn, Brodman had watched him bind himself for prayer in the cold light from the east. When he left the house for work, he remained stooped, like the curve he'd taught Brodman to draw for the Hebrew script. Never had Brodman loved his father more than in those moments, though later he wondered whether what he had taken for love was partly pity, mingled with the desire to protect his father from further pain.

After three months they brought his mother home, and

propped her on pillows with a view of the water stain on the ceiling. The pale-blue skin was stretched taut over her ankles and shone. Brodman cooked for her and fed her, and then studied at the table under the flypaper, listening for her dry coughs. When his father came home, he put the food on the table for him. Afterward he mopped the oilcloth clean and took down the Hebrew books with their crumbling leather spines. His father's lips moved soundlessly, his broad-nailed finger searching out the passage. Abraham bound Isaac once so that Isaac would go on binding himself forever. Each night before bed Brodman checked his bindings, the way a man double-checks the doors and windows of his house. When he left the apartment, he locked the door quietly behind him, and on his back he carried his mother, with her blue ankles, and his stooped father, and their parents, too, dead in a trench at the edge of a pine forest.

But not his daughters. Had they sensed the price he'd paid, and learned from him after all—he with his old books, stunted by duty? All through their childhood, his father's sepia face had looked miserably down on them from the living-room wall. But they were going to have none of it. They had turned and walked briskly away in the opposite direction. They'd thought nothing of rejecting what he cherished. They had not revered him. From Carol he had received only disdain, and from Ruthie indifference. He had been enraged at them for it, but at bottom he'd envied how they stood up for themselves. Only when it was too late did he come to understand that they were no happier than he was, and no more free. At nineteen, Carol had been hospitalized. When he went to her, she was strapped to the bed in a straitjacket. He had underestimated her condition, and taken her a book of stories by Agnon. Embarrassed, he left it clumsily on the table. She looked up at the ceiling, as his mother had once looked up.

Brodman had not suffered such softness of the brain. The gene for it—if that's what it was—had passed over him. Or he had hardened his mind against it. His illness was of the flesh, and could be cut away. Now it was in a lab jar somewhere, after his difficult cesarean, and his grandson was in an incubator, four weeks premature. No, he was not confused, only overwhelmed by the symmetry. Together they convalesced, Brodman on the eleventh floor and his grandson on the sixth. Brodman from death and his grandson from life. Mira hurried between them like a congressional aide. Visitors came and went. For the baby, they brought plush toys and tiny onesies of Egyptian cotton. For Brodman, strained fruit and books that he lacked the concentration to read.

At last, on the day the baby was to be released from the hospital, Brodman was well enough to be brought to him. Early in the morning, the Russian nurse came to give him a sponge bath. "Now we wash to meet grandson!" she sang, going about it with a firm hand. Looking down, he discovered that he no longer had a navel. The mark of his birth had been replaced by an ugly red welt, four inches across. What was he to make of this? The Russian rolled him down the corridor in a wheelchair. Through open doors, he saw the bruised shins and clawed feet of the nearly dead poking from the blankets.

But when he arrived, the room was already filled to capacity with people who had claims on the child—his daughter, her girlfriend, the homosexual who had contributed the sperm, the homosexual's boyfriend. For more than an hour, Brodman waited his turn. From the wheelchair it was impossible even to catch a glimpse of the baby, who was completely walled in by his progenitors. Furious, Brodman wheeled himself out, rode the elevator in the wrong direction, toured the dialysis center, and followed signs to the meditation courtyard, where he took out his anger on a squat and mossy Buddha. When no one came for him, he decided to go back to pick a fight with his daughter.

By the time he returned, the room had emptied out. Mira placed the sleeping baby in his arms, wrapped in white. He held his breath, staring at the whorls of the child's perfect ear, luminescent, as if painted by Fra Filippo Lippi. Afraid of dropping him, Brodman tried to shift the bundle in his arms, but the baby started and opened his sticky, lashless eyes. Brodman felt something being tugged painfully from his decrepit body. He held the boy against his chest and would not let go.

That night he lay in his bed on the eleventh floor, too agitated to sleep. His grandson was at home in his crib now, swaddled in soft things and dreaming under a lightly spinning mobile. *Good, sleep, bubbeleh. All is still quiet in your world, nothing is yet upon you. No one wishes to ask your opinion about anything.* Not that the child was protected from opinions. They swirled around him. Ruthie had asked Mira to buy him a Moses basket. "What does she want with such a basket?" Brodman said. Realizing that she'd steered wrong, Mira wrestled the basket back into the tissue paper. But he had already sunk in his teeth. "How long must we go on reenacting this little charade?" he asked. "We're not slaves in Egypt anymore. What's more, we were never slaves in Egypt."

"You're being ridiculous," Mira said, pushing the basket back into the Saks bag and kicking it under her chair. Brodman knew it and didn't care. He wouldn't give up. "A Moses basket? Why, Mira? Explain it to me."

No, he couldn't sleep. Somewhere in the wide world there must be children who were born and raised without precedent—the idea of it sent a shiver of awe down his spine. Who might he have been, had it been given to him to choose? But his chance had passed. He had allowed himself to be crushed by duty. He had failed to fully become himself, had instead given in to ancient pressures. And now he saw how foolish it had all been, what a waste! Burned brilliant by fever, he had understood everything. The arguments of the dead had been laid out for him, the irreducible proofs of those who knew from the other side. He had died and been called back so that he might instruct the child, and set him on a different path.

In the morning, Mira arrived with buttered rolls sweating in a Ziploc bag. He ate his breakfast and listened to her stories of the child's victorious homecoming, of his powerful pissing and great thirst. Brodman, too, was pissing and drinking volumes, and when the doctor came by on his rounds he joked with Mira that her holiday was almost over. Tomorrow or the next day they would be sending Brodman home. Home—Brodman suddenly remembered it. The endless hours in the dark back room, trying to ignite a broken fuse. Day after day, year after year, the blank legal pad had reproached him with its fine lines. All that was finished now. He hadn't been brought back to life for the sake of absurdity.

The ambulance that drove him home did not use its siren.

Too small by half, the child had not been circumcised at eight days. In the hospital, they had fattened him like Hansel, and at home he continued to enlarge himself. Now the news came that the doctor had given the all-clear. The event would be held in Ruthie's apartment. Bagels and lox would be served. A female mohel who broke with custom to allow for a topical anesthetic had been found in Riverdale. All of this Brodman overheard from the bedroom. When Mira came in to tell him the news, he pretended to be asleep. He was too tired to explain to her the nature of his revelations. The incandescence of his fever had dimmed. The days were clotted with boredom now. Had he not once been a man of action? He had always thought of himself as such, but what proof did he have? The evidence—a meager output of books, themselves commentaries on commentaries on other books—suggested otherwise. Bolstered by foam pillows, he looked up at the thin patch of sky between buildings. Carol was a person of action. Carol had lost her mind and become a person of action. A person who stood up to tanks and bulldozers, who fought for the things she believed in. But he, her father, had kept his mind, and closed himself up in it as a man closes himself up in a faultless argument.

He had shed twenty pounds during his ordeal, and his clothes no longer fit him. Busy with catering and the folding chairs, Mira had failed to think of this until two hours before the bris. Brodman shouted, though it still hurt to shout, and threatened to go in his stained robe. Mira, who for fifty years had met his temper with implacable calm, continued to field phone calls while packing up platters. Then she left the apartment without a word. Brodman heard the door close, and stoked his rage with the thought that she had left without him. He was about to pick up the phone to scream at Ruthie when Mira returned with a maroon silk shirt and brown pants from the upstairs neighbor, whose wife she sometimes had coffee with. Disgusted, Brodman tossed the silk shirt onto the floor and roared. But soon the anger went out of him like the heat in a house with old windows, leaving only helplessness and despair. Twenty minutes later, he was standing downstairs, in ballooning silk sleeves, while the doorman hailed a cab.

It was winter now. The taxi made its way through the gray streets of the city where Brodman had lived all his life. Buildings smeared past the fogged window. Mira had nothing to say to him. In the lobby of Ruthie's place, he stood waiting in borrowed clothes, surrounded by Mira's plastic bags. She had ridden up in the elevator to get help. Brodman thought of turning to go. He pictured himself making his way home through the chilly streets.

Seventeen years ago, after his father died, Brodman had been sideswiped by a debilitating depression. It was a black period, and at the bottom of it he had thought seriously of taking his life. Only after his father was gone did Brodman discover what his powerful presence had obscured. An ambivalence, like a fault line, that now threatened to topple everything that had been built over it. No, more than ambivalence. An objection. Not to his father, whom he had loved. But to what his father had asked of him, just as it had been asked of his father, and his father before that, and back and back through the chain of relentless begetting. No, he was not angry! he bellowed in the therapist's office. "I simply object to the burden!"

"Of what?" she asked, pen poised, waiting to copy it down in his file.

After a month, the insomnia and the migraines stopped, and he began slowly to recognize himself again. For months afterward, he was shaken every time he remembered how close he had come to giving up. Inhaling the smell of fresh horseshit in Central Park, seeing the skyscrapers loom up above the tree line, he felt overcome with gratitude. The museums along Fifth Avenue, the yellow taxis in sunlight, music—these things made his knees weak, as if he had just safely crawled back from a ledge. Finding himself in front of Carnegie Hall, or one of the dazzled theaters on Broadway right as the audience spilled out, still abroad in another world, Brodman felt embraced by life. The bitter taste of his objection had passed. But some part of him had gone with it. He had been damaged by the dissent, and could never again be what he had been. It must have been then that it began: the slow drain of understanding that dried up his once fertile mind.

In the dingy lobby of his daughter's building, leaning on his hospital-issued cane, he watched the numbers above the elevator light up in descending order. The doors parted to reveal the smiling face of the sperm donor. "Grandpa!" he called sonorously, and pumped Brodman's hand before sweeping up the shopping bags. In the close elevator, Brodman began to sweat. He breathed through his mouth so as to avoid inhaling the man's overripe cologne. The elevator rumbled up through the floors, carrying all the male relatives the poor child had in the world. Brodman winced, trying to shut out an image of the man beside him diddling with himself to fill a paper cup.

The apartment was already crowded with people. One of Ruthie's oldest friends accosted Brodman and kissed him dryly on the cheek. "It's good to see you home again. You gave everyone a scare," she said, loudly, as if his illness had also deafened him. Brodman grunted, and made his way to the window. He wrenched it open and inhaled the cold air. But when he turned back to the overfilled apartment, he was lightheaded. Across the room, Mira was busy coaxing tea from a large samovar for the mohelet from Riverdale. This woman, with her crocheted kippa the size of a dinner plate, had arrived in a prepaid sedan to remove his grandson's foreskin as a mark of God's covenant. To cut away his flesh, so that the child's soul should not be cut off forever from his people.

Brodman felt unsteady on his feet. He pushed his way through the kitchen, past the tubs of cream cheese under plastic wrap, and thumped down the dark corridor with the metal cane. He wanted only to lie down in Ruthie's bedroom and close his eyes. But when he opened the door, he found the bed occupied by a mountain of coats and scarves. Hot tears sprang to his eyes. He felt a howl building in his lungs, the howl of a man who has been shut out by grace. But what he heard instead was a soft gurgle. He spun around and saw the reed basket in the corner, tucked next to a rocking chair. The baby opened his tiny mouth. For a moment it seemed he might cry out, or even speak. But instead he lifted a tiny mottled fist and tried to shove it inside. Brodman moved toward him, filled with feeling. Sensing a change in his world of light and shadow, the baby turned. Wide-eyed, he regarded his grandfather with a questioning look. Down the hall, they were preparing the yoke and the blade. How could he help the boy now?

The service door led to the fire stairs. Abandoning the cane, Brodman clutched the bannister and dragged himself up two flights. His stomach muscles ached. Three times he had to put the basket down to catch his breath. At last they reached the top, and Brodman pushed the metal bar of the door that released them to the roof.

Birds exploded from the ledge, soaring skyward. Below, the city spread out in all directions. From here it appeared quiet, almost still. To the west, he saw the great barges on the Hudson, the cliffs of faraway New Jersey. Heaving, he set the basket down on the tar paper. The baby squirmed in the cold; his eyes blinked with wonder. Brodman trembled with love for him. His beautiful features were wholly unfamiliar, loyal to no one. A child still without measure, equal only to himself. Perhaps he would turn out not to resemble any of them.

They would already have discovered him missing below. Alarms would be ringing, the apartment in chaos. Brodman felt the wind knife through the silk shirt. He had no plan. If he had hoped for some guidance, there was none to be found here. The leaden sky had sealed the heavens up. Stooping with difficulty, he lifted the baby out of the basket. His tiny head flopped back, but Brodman caught it and cradled it tenderly in the crook of his arm. He rocked and swayed gently, just as his father had in the early morning, after he had wrapped the black straps around his arm and head. If he was weeping, he did not know it. He stroked the baby's soft cheek with his finger. The boy's gray eyes seemed to look on him with patience. But Brodman could not say what it was that he was meant to tell the child. Restored to life, he could no longer parse the infinite wisdom of the dead.

I Am Asleep but My Heart Is Awake

Asleep in my father's apartment, I dream that someone is at the door. It's him—he is three, or maybe four, years old. He's crying; I don't know why, only that he is bitterly disappointed. I try to distract him by showing him a picture book with beautiful illustrations, in colors far brighter than those one gets in life. He glances at the book, but carries on anyway. In his eyes I see that everything has already been decided. So instead I pick him up and carry him around on my hip. It isn't easy, but that's how it has to be, because he's so upset, this tiny father-child.

The latch of the front door awakens me. I've been living here alone for more than a week. Now, lying still, I listen to the sound of footsteps entering, and a bag being set heavily on the floor. The footsteps move away, toward the small kitchen, and I hear the creak of the cabinet open and close. The sound of water rushing from the tap. Whoever it is knows his way, so there is no one it can be.

From the bedroom doorway I see the stranger's broad, stooped back. It takes up half the tiny kitchen. He gulps down a glass of water, fills it again, drains that one, and a third. Then he rinses the glass and places it to dry, upside down, on the rack. He's sweated through his white shirt. He unbuttons the sleeves and rolls them to the elbows. He splashes his face with water, removes the checked dishcloth from the peg, dries himself brusquely, and stops to press the towel into his eyes. From his back pocket he produces a small comb and runs it through his hair, smoothing it into place. When he turns, his face is not the face I expected, although there was no face I was expecting. This face is old and refined, with a long nose and high, flared nostrils. His eyes are hooded, but surprisingly light and nimble. He walks the few steps back into the living room, tosses his wallet on the table, and only then, looking up, does he notice me watching him from the doorway.

MY FATHER IS dead; he died two months ago. At the hospital in New York I was given his clothes, his watch, and the book he'd been reading as he ate alone at the restaurant. I searched his pockets for a note to me, first the pants and then the raincoat. Finding none, I read the book, about legal theory and Maimonides. I couldn't make sense of the words. I had not prepared myself for his death. He had not prepared me. My mother died when I was three. We had already dealt with death, in our way we'd agreed to be finished with it. Then, without warning, my father broke our agreement.

A few days after the shiva, Koren brought me the keys to the apartment in Tel Aviv. I hadn't known there was anything that belonged to my father there. In the five years before he died, he had taught the winter semester in Israel, in the city where he grew up. But I always assumed that he lived in rooms loaned to him by the university, the sort of spare, impersonal place visiting academics are always given, which have everything and nothing: salt in the cupboard, but never olive oil; a knife, but a knife that doesn't cut. He told me almost nothing about where he lived between January and May. But he was not secretive about it. I knew, for example, that he stayed in the center and commuted to the campus in Ramat Aviv three times a week because he preferred the city, and that the apartment where he stayed was not far from the sea, where he liked to walk in the early morning. When we spoke on the phone, as we often did, and he told me about the concerts he attended, the dishes he had tried cooking, and the book he was writing, I never pictured his surroundings on the other end of the line. And when I tried to recall those conversations, it seemed to me that there was nothing beyond the sound of my father's voice: it absorbed even the need to imagine.

And yet there was Koren, with the keys to the apartment I hadn't known of. It was Koren, the executor of my father's will, who'd taken care of the funeral arrangements; I had only to be present when they lowered him into the ground, to add the first shovel of dirt. The hollow thud it made on the pine casket made my knees buckle. Standing in the cemetery in a dress too heavy for the warm weather, I remembered the one time I'd seen him drunk. He and Koren had sung so loudly it had woken me up: *Chad gadya, chad gadya. One little goat, one little goat. The dog came, and bit the cat, that ate the goat, that my father bought for two zuzim.* Once my father told me that the Torah contained no mention of the everlasting soul—that the soul as we know it came along only in the Talmud, and, like all technological advances, it made things easier but cut people off from something that had once been native to them. What was he saying? That the invention of the soul made people strangers to death? Or was he instructing me not to think of him as a soul once he was gone?

Koren copied the address onto the back of his business card and told me that my father had wanted me to have the apartment. Afterward, as we stood in the fluorescent-lit hall waiting for his elevator, sensing, perhaps, that he had not adequately conveyed some message, Koren added, "He thought it was someplace you might go sometimes."

Why? Why, when all these years I'd never visited him there, nor had he ever invited me? I had cousins in the north of the country but was rarely in touch with them; their mother, my father's sister, was nothing like him. My cousins are hard, practical, unsparing people. Now they already have children of their own whom they let run freely in the street, playing with sharp and rusty things. I admire them but don't know how to speak to them. After my grandmother died, when I was ten, I'd only gone back once. There was no longer any reason to go. As if something had been decided, my father gave up speaking to me in Hebrew. I'd been answering him in English for years, and so I hardly noticed, but later I came to sense that the language he still dreamed in was an argument he had lost with someone else, not me.

NOW WHEN THE stranger in my father's apartment speaks to me, I answer reflexively in English: "I'm Adam's daughter. Who are you?"

"You surprised me," he says, clapping his chest. He sinks down onto the sofa, his knees falling open.

"You're a friend of my father?"

"Yes," he says, rubbing his throat under the open collar. The hair on his chest is sparse and gray. He gestures for me to sit, as if it were I who had appeared unannounced in his living room, and not vice versa. With shining eyes, he takes me in. "I should have guessed, you look like him. Only prettier."

"You didn't say your name."

"Boaz."

My father had never mentioned a Boaz.

"I'm an old friend," the stranger says.

"Why do you have the keys?"

"He lets me use the place when he isn't here. Now and then, when I come through the city. I stay in the back bedroom, and check on things for him. Last month there was a leak from up-stairs."

"My father died."

For a moment he says nothing. I can feel him studying me.

"I know." He stands up, turning his back to me, and easily lifts the heavy bag of groceries he'd set down earlier. But instead of leaving, as I expect—as any normal person would—he retreats to the kitchen. "I'm making something to eat," he says without turning. "If you're hungry, it'll be ready in fifteen minutes."

From the living room I watch him nimbly chopping the vegetables, cracking the eggs, and rummaging in the refrigerator. It annoys me to see him making himself so at home. My father is gone, and yet this stranger intends to take advantage of his hospitality. But I haven't eaten all day.

"Sit," he commands, sliding the omelet from the skillet onto my plate. Obediently, I take my place, just as I used to do when my father called me to the table. I eat quickly, without seeming to taste the food, so as not to give him any pleasure—although it's good, the best I've had in a long time. My father used to say that food tasted better to him when I ate it, but it also always tasted better to me when he'd prepared it. I pick the last salad leaves off the plate with my fingers, and when I look up, the stranger is watching me with pale green eyes.

"Your hair," he says, "you always wear it so short?" I shoot him a look to make it clear that I have no interest in getting personal. He eats in silence for a few minutes before trying again: "You're a student?"

I drink my water without bothering to correct him. Through the bottom of the glass I see his blurred mouth.

He tells me that he is an engineer. "Then you can afford to stay wherever you want when you come to the city," I say. He stops chewing and smiles, revealing small, gray, childish teeth. "I work for the municipal department," he says, and names a city in the north. "Anyway, this is the most convenient."

It makes no difference to him, whoever he is, that my father has died—why should he let that get in the way of convenience?

I decide to tell him to leave right now. I push back my chair and drop my plate in the sink, but what I find myself saying, instead, is that I am going out for a walk.

"Good," he says, and goes on chewing in a slow manner, his fork and knife poised delicately in the air above his plate. "Get some fresh air. I'll do the dishes."

IT'S LATE IN the afternoon, but the heat hasn't let up. All the same, my annoyance dissipates once I'm outside. On the taxi ride from the airport I'd been surprised by how ugly and run-down everything looked, the pockmarked walls and rusted rebar poking from concrete columns on the roofs. But now I'm already used to it. It even comforts me in a way, this lazy decrepitude, along with the dusty trees, the yellow sunlight, and the sound of my father's language.

Soon I come to the water. I sit cross-legged on the beach and choose a small piece of the sea to watch, a tiny piece that changes with the light and the wind and some force far below. A child is sitting at the shore's edge, shouting with glee every time the waves lap her legs, while her parents sit in plastic chairs, talking and sharing a thermos of coffee. It's easy enough to understand what drew my father back here. More difficult to understand is why he stayed away for twenty years. He left with me after my mother died. He got a job teaching in New York, I started school, and we spoke less and less about my mother's absence, or our lives before. I became a native, but he could only ever be a foreigner, and now that I am here, in his city, I wonder for the first time why he waited so long to return, after I'd already grown up and finished college. When I first opened the door of the apartment I hadn't known about, I was overwhelmed by what I found: the walls lined with books, the faded rugs my father must have hunted for in the market, his opera records, the baubles on the shelves, mementos from his travels, the tin tea caddies and the colorful dishes in the cabinet, the battered upright piano with Bach still open on the stand. Even the smell of spices in the kitchen. It was my father's place, there was no question of that; here were all of the things he loved. But it was exactly this thoroughness that surprised and unsettled me. It was as if I was looking at my father's life upside down: *this* was his real home, and the apartment I'd grown up in was merely the place he stayed when away from here. Standing in the middle of his living room, I felt a stab of betrayal. If there were such thing as a soul, however refracted, to where would his return?

BY THE TIME I get back to my father's street, it's already dusk, and I see the lights on in his apartment. My eye catches something moving on the washing line that extends from the bathroom window. Some shirts—*my* shirts—are swaying in the shadows. I follow the cord until my gaze arrives at a pair of large hands, delicately pinning my underwear up to dry.

Racing up the two flights of stairs, I bang the light switch in the hall, fumble with the keys, and fly through the door. "What are you doing?" I explode, gasping for breath, the blood buzzing in my ears. "Who gave you the right to go through my things?"

The municipal engineer has stripped to his white undershirt. The basket of wet clothes is balanced on the stool beside him.

"They were on top of the washing machine. I stained my shirt cooking, and it seemed a waste to run a wash for nothing."

He places a clothespin between his thick lips and turns back to the careful work of pinning my clothes and letting out the line. His shoulders are covered with the sunspots that come with age, but his arms are thick and muscular. He wears no wedding ring.

"Listen," I say in a low voice, though he is already listening. "I don't know who you are, but you can't just go letting yourself into people's apartments and invading their privacy."

He puts down the clothes and removes the pin from his mouth. "Have I invaded your privacy?"

"You're going through my underwear!"

"And you think they interest me?"

Now the heat rushes to my face. The pair of purple underwear that was in his hands a moment ago is old and childish, the elastic stretched out.

"That's not what I'm saying."

"So what are you saying? You don't want me to do your laundry? Next time I won't." He pins the last shirt and turns away from the window. "There's ice cream in the refrigerator. I'm going out and I won't be back until late. There's no need to wait up for me; I have the key. In case you have nowhere to go, there's a good movie on at nine."

WHY DO I watch the movie? I eat the ice cream and watch the movie, just as he suggested. The movie isn't half bad, it's true, but I fall asleep anyway, and when I wake up something else is on. It's past midnight. I put my father's watch to my ear. It will go on ticking for only so long, and soon the surplus of time he left for me will be spent. But for now it goes on ticking.

Somewhere there is a cat crying, or maybe a baby. I run the water for a bath and, lying back, I notice for the first time a dark water stain on the ceiling where the plaster has begun to peel from a leak. Before I go to bed, I knock on the door of the tiny back bedroom, although I know he isn't there: I would have heard him come in. I flip the light switch. The narrow bed is as neatly made as a soldier's. He seems too big for such a bed—my bed, it suddenly occurs to me, the one my father meant for me to sleep in if I'd ever come to visit. But I had not visited, and so in the meantime the small bed had been loaned out to a stranger.

There is a wooden dresser at the foot of the bed, the only other piece of furniture that fits in the room. Opening the top drawer, I find a shaving kit, toothbrush, and a change of underwear. The others are empty.

In my father's bedroom, I take out the small leather photo album I found in the drawer of his night table. In the apartment where I grew up, the only photographs my father kept were of me, and now, since I found the little album a week ago, I can't stop looking at it. On the first page is a picture of him as a young man, even younger than I am now. He wears shorts and hiking boots, and stands in front of the rock wall of a canyon. It's uncanny how much the face in the photo looks like mine. Though we always shared a resemblance, it was muted by the difference in our ages. But in this picture it's easy to see how it happens— how one nose gets passed down through time; one set of ears that stick out a little too much; one eye that is just the tiniest bit smaller than the other, as if to hold itself back from seeing. Even our postures are similar, as if we were born, one after the other, to occupy the same spot.

It takes me a moment to pick him out in the next photo. He's swimming in a pool under a waterfall with some others, mouth open, eyes laughing, the shutter snapped just as he was shouting to the person behind the lens. In the third photo he's crouching on a rock, shirtless, a cigarette cupped in his hand, a girl next to him, her legs outstretched. Now the familiarity of his face, which is also my face, begins to feel even stranger, because this relaxed young man has so little to do with my father, who was disciplined and rigorous even in the pursuit of his pleasures. In the last photo, his arms are thrown out, and he is laughing in a desert that stretches behind him forever. It fills me with longing, as if I, too, had been there long ago, or as if part of me goes on being there, or maybe it's just the feeling that I would give anything to meet him there, to stand face-to-face with him, a mirror image of the desert stretching behind me forever.

I FALL ASLEEP without realizing it, and when I open my eyes again a filmy dawn fills the window, and I have the sense that something has woken me. In the dream I was having, many people were coming and going from a place that was supposedly my father's apartment, but actually looked more like the train station of a small town. I understood that my father was dying there, in the stationmaster's office, like Tolstoy. I get up for a glass of water, and in the hall I see that the door of the spare bedroom is slightly ajar. When I push it open, a heavy odor drifts out, the odor of a man's body abandoned to sleep. I see him sunk into the covers, legs thrown over the edge, arms wrapped around the pillow, breathing evenly. Submerged in sleep, given over entirely to it, as if he no longer had any responsibility left in the world but to sleep like that—to sleep the sleep of the dead. I feel myself growing drowsy just watching him. As if his sleep has cast a spell over me, suddenly my limbs feel heavy and all I want is to collapse back into bed, to burrow down in the blankets and abandon myself to a long and dreamless sleep. I'm so exhausted that if the bed in the small room hadn't been so narrow I'd have crawled in next to him, curled up, and closed my eyes. I have to fight to pull myself away and back down the hall, and when I get there I fall into bed.

When I finally rouse myself, it's already noon, and sunlight streams through the slats of the shutters. The long blind sleep has left me agitated and restless. The door of the small bedroom is closed. I walk all the way to the pool on the roof of Dizengoff Center, a large mall with cheap clothing shops and a movie theater. The women with saggy-bottomed bathing suits drift back and forth, and the old man with the gold swimming cap is there again, doing his knee bends in the shallow end. If he slips below the surface and doesn't come up, the lifeguard will come down and fish him out, but once he leaves and goes home there are no lifeguards. One day he will slip below the surface in his own house, or on the street, the way my father slipped below the surface in a restaurant. Or maybe it isn't like that at all—maybe the weights that hold life down suddenly lift.

I swim thirty lengths, then walk back to the apartment. The door of the stranger's bedroom is still closed. I make some toast and afterward go out to read at a nearby café, where the waiter in skinny jeans with a lazy eye smiles at me while he squeezes my orange juice. Afterward I wander through the market. A man tries to sell me a hat, but I don't want a hat. What do I want? the man wants to know. I go to the beach and watch the hairy men playing paddleball. By the time I return to my father's apartment, it's already late in the afternoon, the shadows on the sidewalk grow away from the sea, and the municipal engineer is in the kitchen baking stuffed peppers. Only at that moment, the moment I come through the door and see him peering into the oven, does it occur to me that my father might have arranged this. That just as he had prepared his will, given Koren the keys, and made sure his wish for me to come here was communicated, my father might also have gone to the trouble of asking his old friend to watch over me, or to pass something on to me, however discreetly, some message or sign of what to do now that he was gone.

"You're back," he says, lowering the volume of the news from the radio. "Good. Dinner is almost ready. You like cherries? The grocer had cherries today."

I want to ask him where he was last night. I want to ask about the undertow that pulled me out with him into fathomless sleep. But what would be the question? Instead I set the table and wonder which chair my father used to sit in. I decide it must have been the one closest to the stove, facing the window—the one Boaz sat in yesterday. This time when we sit to share the meal he has prepared, he in his chair and I in mine, I make a point of being more friendly. Something has changed, and he knows it. His nimble eyes, even lighter than I'd remembered, regard me with a questioning look, and something else, too, a kind of sad patience. I wish he would talk, but he carries on eating in silence. It's up to me to speak, so I tell him that I'm not in fact a student, that I've been working in an architecture firm for three years, but that I don't like it. When I wake up in the morning, I tell him, I don't look forward to the hours in front of the computer, the architect's bad-tempered outbursts, and the complaints of his rich clients.

"So why do you stay?" he asks, wiping his mouth.

AFTER DINNER HE takes a bath, and in my room I hear the water ripple each time he moves on the other side of the wall. Twenty minutes later he comes out of the bathroom dressed in the same clothes, freshly shaved, his wet hair neatly slicked back.

"I'm going out for a while," he says, "so you'll have the place to yourself." He goes down the hall to the small bedroom, carrying his toothbrush and his towel. I can smell his aftershave in the humid air that floats out of the bathroom.

"What did you come here for?" I blurt out when he appears again. It isn't the way I'd meant to ask, and immediately I regret it. I want him to know that I understand the need to uphold our parts in the charade we're playing for my father's sake. And so quickly I add, "Just to check for leaks?"

"To see someone," he answers, and by the way he says it, shoving his hands into his pockets, I sense that it's a woman. For the second time I'm surprised at myself, at the way his answer disappoints me. It was not what I'd expected him to say—though what was it that I'd expected him to say? That he came for me?

And I surprise myself yet again when, a few moments after he goes out the front door, I slip out after him and hurry down the stairs. I follow him at a distance down the street. He passes under a mulberry tree, so I pass. He crosses to the other side, so

I cross. He stops to look up at the tall building they are raising, and I too stop to look up, and it seems to me that I could go on doing this for a very long time, shadowing a life.

Soon we are in an unfamiliar part of the city, more run-down than the rest. The terraces seem to be hanging on by a few screws. He stops at a bakery and comes out again holding a small box tied with string. Cookies? What kind? Cakes? The woman's favorite kind, which she waits for every time, and has come to expect? He looks across the street, and for an instant it seems that his eyes catch mine. But his face registers nothing, and he turns away and continues to walk. A few blocks farther, he goes into a supermarket, and this time I wait behind a car until I see him come out with a plastic bag.

By now it's dark. The stranger, Boaz—if that's his name—is still moving up ahead. We walk for almost an hour. But I don't mind, I've always been a good walker. My father used to say that even as a little girl I would walk very far and never complain. If it weren't for my thirst, and the fact that I ran out without my wallet, I'd be content to go on like this all night. But soon I'm really dying for a drink, and every time we pass one of the wire recycling cages filled with the negative shapes of so many quenched thirsts, I'm reminded.

At last the stranger stops in front of a squat stucco apartment building. The small front garden is overgrown, crowded by a large bush by the entrance and a wild-looking tree whose dark, glossy leaves partly obscure the facade. He pauses to look up, and through the leaves I see that the windows of the first floor are lit up. He goes through the front gate, but instead of enter-ing the building he walks around to the side alley, and four or five skinny cats spill out of the bushes, threading through his legs and purring as he removes some tins from the supermarket bag. He peels off the tops and sets the tins down on the ground. The cats swarm, more appearing from under the bushes. When he kicks some empty tins aside, they leap back and tense. He says something to calm them, and they return to devouring the food. I stand under the streetlamp, no longer caring if he sees me. But if he knows I'm there, he doesn't let on. Stuffing the plastic bag into his pocket, he comes back around to the front and pauses, as if to sniff something in the night air, and looks up again at the lit windows through the leaves. The branches move in the breeze, tapping the glass, and he stands, jingling the coins and keys in his pocket, as if trying to decide something that could go either way. Then, squaring his shoulders, he hurries up the path and disappears into the dark lobby. A cat yowls, somewhere a television is on, but otherwise it's quiet. For a moment I think I can hear the waves, but it's only the breeze rising in the leaves. I cross to the other side of the empty street, but it's even harder to see into the windows from there. It's obvious I'll have to climb the tree.

Standing at the base of the trunk, I search for a foothold and manage to hoist myself up into the branches. The twigs catch on my T-shirt, and the resin that oozes out of the broken stems makes my hands sticky. Once my foot slips, and I almost fall. But then I am high enough, and close enough, that I can almost reach out and touch them: a young woman and a child, sitting peacefully at a table, framed in a rectangle of light. Her long hair is braided down her back, and when she looks up from her book to see what the child has drawn, I see her light-colored

eyes, and the thought comes to me—calmly, clearly—that somewhere, somehow, someone has given him the wrong key, and
that she is the daughter he has come back to watch over. Legs
trembling from effort, I grip the tree trunk, waiting for her to
hear the doorbell and to let him in. What could be taking him
so long? What is he rehearsing on the other side of her door?
And is it only their own doors, the doors of those they love,
that become locked to the dead?

At that moment I hear footsteps below, and see him hurrying underneath into the street. The twigs tear past on my way
down, scratching my face and arms. I jump the last part, land
hard, and begin to run. At the top of the block I see a figure
turn the corner, but by the time I get there there's no sign of
him, and the quiet street ends in a wide and busy avenue. Traffic
speeds past. A bus groans to a halt, and it seems possible he's on
the other side of it, but when it pulls away the sidewalk is empty.
I look into the only place that's open, an all-night pharmacy on
the corner, but there is only an old woman leaning on her cane
among the boxes and bottles, patiently waiting for her prescrip-
tion to be filled. How could he have just disappeared like that?
I think, angry at him and at myself. Though maybe the real
question is how I managed to follow him so far.

NO PLACE IN TEL AVIV is ever far from the sea, and when I
find my way to it and get my bearings, I realize I'm closer to
my father's apartment than I'd thought. The sea is different in
the dark, more vast and alive, filled with intelligence. When I
get to the rock jetty behind the old shuttered discotheque, I see
a group of men casting their fishing lines off the end into the

black water. I watch for a while, but nothing comes of it. I wonder whether I should go home and wait for the stranger. But I feel he won't come back, not tonight, and not tomorrow either, just as I also feel that a decade will pass, and I'll have children of my own, before I finally change the lock.

By the time I return, it's past midnight. I check the stranger's room, but it's empty, as I knew it would be, the bed neatly made. My head feels heavy, and a feeling of exhaustion comes over me. I strip off my clothes, dropping them in a trail in the hallway on my way to bed, as I've always done when I've lived alone. The shutters are closed, and I inch through the pitch-dark and collapse on top of the covers. Only then, lying still with my eyes open, do I hear the rhythmic breath of someone already asleep in the bed. I scream out, arms flailing, and my fist sinks into something soft and warm. I grope for the lamp, and when the bulb flares, I see the stranger sprawled out in his undershirt, mouth half open, abandoned to sleep just as before. He couldn't have gotten home long before me, and yet he's already so far from the shore of wakefulness that neither my scream nor my fist has roused him. Heart pounding, I snatch my T-shirt from the floor and throw it over my head. I mean to shake him awake and demand an explanation for everything, to tell him to get out of my bed, or my father's bed—at the very least a bed that isn't his, for his is down the hall if it is anywhere at all. But just as I'm about to grab him by the shoulders, a powerful chill comes over me. Suddenly I'm afraid to disturb him, as if he might have been sleepwalking all this time, as if waking him might unsettle a balance, causing something to cease or fall still forever.

I switch off the lamp, close the door gently behind me, go down the hall to the spare bedroom, and climb into the narrow bed. For a while it seems that sleep will never come, until I open my eyes and it's morning, and I hear the sound of the bath running. But it isn't the bath; it's the sound of water rushing through the pipes in the wall from the apartment above. Perhaps soon there will be another leak, and then the stranger will have to wake up and deal with it. I get out of bed and go to look for him in my father's bedroom. The door is open and the bed is empty, the sheets unmade. Entering the living room, I almost trip over him. He's curled up on the floor, legs pulled into his stomach, hands tucked between his knees, sleeping like a baby. Very gently, I prod him with my foot, but he carries on serenely, untouched in his vast sleep. How long can this go on? I wonder. Soon winter will come, the sea will darken, and the rain will fall, leaving puddles in the broken asphalt. But even as I think this, I know in my heart that it will go on a very long time. That I will get used to stepping over the stranger on my way to the kitchen because that is the way one lives, casually stepping over such things until they are no longer a burden to us, and it is possible to forget them altogether.

End Days

On the third day of the fires, after they jumped the borders and entered the city, the rabbi called to find out if her parents' judgment of divorce had arrived. The telephone woke Noa. It was barely past seven, but the rabbi had probably been awake since dawn, his world a more ancient place. She put him on hold while she got up and searched through the stacks of mail that had piled up since Leonard and Monica left. Under the bills and advertisements, she found the thick brown envelope from the California State Supreme Court.

"Hello?" she said into the phone. "It's here."

Her finger must have slipped, because now the rabbi's voice flooded forth on speakerphone, magnified and amplified, with instructions on how to deliver him a copy, so that the get—the Jewish divorce agreement—could be finalized and officially registered. She copied down the address. The rabbi was leading a trip to Poland, flying tomorrow with a group of thirty-five. Before he departed for the camps and ghettos, he wanted to get this squared away. "That everything should be in order," he told her. And so the paperwork in Noa's hand was needed immediately. Today if possible; tomorrow morning at the latest. The rabbi made no mention of the fires. They had nothing to do with him, burning now and here.

COME SUMMER, NOA'S family, too, had always gone back in time. Back three thousand years, to the Iron Age and its successive disasters. Leonard liked to say that they were profiting from other people's tragedies. Her father never failed to deliver this line every June, when the new team assembled for his welcoming remarks, so that she came to associate the arrival of summer—of stifling heat, of heaped-up time—with the coopting of a distant suffering. Archaeology, Leonard liked to say, is the reverse of building up: as the work descends, it undoes and destroys. And though Noa always looked for a tinge of regret in his voice, she never found it. Once, when she was ten, she had been present at a discussion between him and his second-in-command, an archaeologist named Yuval, who had a three-legged dog. Yuval was agonizing over a small intact wall that he didn't want to destroy. "You think you'll ever remember this wall?" her father demanded. Yuval rubbed the sweat from his forehead with the back of his dirt-caked hand. "Knock it down," her father ordered, and trudged off into the shattering sunlight.

Leonard had been excavating Megiddo since before the

girls were born. Megiddo, called Armageddon by the Greeks, prophesied in the book of Revelation as the place where armies will gather to battle at end times. But its past went back millennia. Over the course of twenty years, Leonard had dug down through the centuries until he'd hit on the tenth, BC, when, according to biblical history, Israel to the north and Judah to the south had been joined together by King David. Megiddo, Leonard liked to say, was the playground for the big questions about the United Kingdom of Israel. But it had been her playground, too, as every year she had spent the summer watched over by the students, who took turns entertaining her and Rachel until they were old enough to entertain themselves. Then they would spend their days reading paperbacks on the dry lawn at the kibbutz where they lived during the excavation, or swimming in its pool, where chlorine stung their eyes and blurred their vision.

But now Rachel was doing an internship in New York, Monica was in Europe taking care of her own ailing mother, and Leonard had returned to Megiddo alone. Alone, too, Noa slid open the patio door and sniffed the air. The acrid smell of burning was at odds with the buoyant morning sun that drifted through the leaves. Just past seven meant that in Megiddo it would already be five in the afternoon, the hour they began washing the load of pottery shards exhumed that day. At five thirty sharp Leonard would arrive, and the team would pour out basket after basket for his inspection, which he would rapidly sift through, deciding what should be sent to Reconstruction, and what should be discarded. She'd watched the procedure countless times when she was younger, positioning herself near enough to snatch a rejected piece off the table, a terra-cotta handle or enameled shard that she could salvage from the trash.

HAVING RAISED TWO daughters and been through thick and thin, Leonard and Monica had separated amicably in early spring. The explanation they gave to those who asked and many who didn't was that after twenty-five years of marriage they were ready for new adventures. What these adventures entailed neither would say, but it was clear to Noa that their terrain would be human rather than geographical. Liberal and evolved as they were, neither saw any great tragedy in their uncoupling, for they would always be friends, Leonard and Monica explained. So amicably did they separate that they had brought Noa and Rachel to the ceremony for the get, required for a Jewish divorce. Brought the girls, as they had once brought them to see a healing dance performed by the San tribe in Namibia, and the changing of the guards at Buckingham Palace. Monica, impeccable as always, wore a floral dress. Rachel came home from college specially, arriving from the East Coast the day before. The divorce had come as a surprise to them both, but only Rachel was convinced that something had happened to instigate it. Noa would have liked to believe that—to believe that only recent events had been hidden from them, rather than a fundamental truth that went back many years. On the drive there, she listened to their parents run though a litany of stories about how they'd met and the early years when the girls were babies, just as the canonical stories about Leonard's mother had been recited at her shiva the year before.

Her parents had let lapse their membership at the synagogue soon after Noa's bat mitzvah, at which she sang tunelessly of Jacob's dream to a roomful of dry eyes. So a rabbi had to be rustled up who could undo the Orthodox wedding they'd had at the insistence of her mother's Viennese parents a quarter century before. His hole-in-the-wall synagogue had once been beautiful, but over the years had fallen into disrepair. The roof had problems, said the young rabbi who let them in, when he saw Monica peering up at the peeling plaster and the stained-glass skylight covered with plastic sheeting. His sparse blond beard barely covered his cheeks; he couldn't have been much older than twenty and did not seem experienced enough to un-ravel her parents' long and complicated marriage. Rabbi Shem-kin was on the way, the young rabbi explained, he was only the assistant. This last statement he directed at Noa, as if sensing her distrust.

The four of them sat in a row on a hard bench in the sanc-tuary while the young rabbi arranged a table and chairs. A back door stood open to a room where children's toys and books were strewn across the floor. They didn't believe in tidying up, these people, Leonard said. Order would be found only in the world to come. He absently tapped his foot while Monica commented on the stained glass. He was wearing nice shoes, and he hated nice shoes, preferred to stride through life in his rough hik-ing boots dusted with the Iron Age. The nice shoes that stiffly held his feet were a nod to a disagreement between her parents that had grown like a stalactite over the years, fed by a distant, mysterious source until it had come to hang like a dagger over their heads.

At last Rabbi Shemkin arrived in his black suit, followed by a fat, slovenly scribe wearing a tallis draped over his white shirt and clutching a ragged portfolio under one arm. Behind him trailed a tall and skinny rabbi with a biblical beard, who would serve as a witness.

"Good!" Rabbi Shemkin exclaimed, clapping his hands together. "Everyone is here."

Leonard moved to take a seat next to Monica at the table, but Rabbi Shemkin clucked his tongue and motioned to the place opposite Noa's mother. Clearing his throat, Leonard strode to the other side of the table. Noa stood with Rachel until the young rabbi hurried forward and ushered them into the front pew.

"Jesus," Rachel muttered under her breath when her flip-flop snagged on the leg of a chair.

Photocopies were passed out with a script for Leonard and Monica to read. Jews had been performing this procedure for two thousand years! the rabbi announced with a smile. Two thousand years of acrimony! Noa added mentally. The scribe opened his portfolio and removed a large feather. With a retractable blade he began to sharpen the nib, the keratin scrapings falling into the folds of his shirt. When Leonard announced that he had a few questions, the scribe plucked a whole handful of feathers out of the portfolio and set to work on these. What kind of feathers were they? Monica asked politely. Turkey, the scribe reported. The tall, lanky witness purred appreciatively, and concurred that turkey was the strongest. The scribe took out a piece of paper and a board strung with gut. Whose gut? Noa wanted to ask. When he pressed the paper over the board and rubbed it with his hand, the page was creased with straight lines. These were used to guide his careful writing of the Hebrew letters that would undo what their parents had decided, without consulting them, that they no longer wanted done. While the scribe wrote, her mother made conversation. She would feel the need to make conversation at a beheading, too. Did she hear him say that his father had been a scribe before him?

"Four generations."

"And maybe before that, you don't know," said Rabbi Shemkin.

"Before that they were butchers."

"First they were slaughtering animals," said the witness, observing the scribe's work, "and now they slaughter people."

"No," said the scribe, not lifting his eyes from the lettering. "Now we're helping people get on with their lives."

When the writing was complete, it was checked and double-checked and read aloud twice by Rabbi Shemkin and the witness. Then they sat waiting for the ink to dry.

"It's a hundred percent humidity today," the witness said, shaking his head at the window. The bunch of keys on the ring clipped to his belt jingled whenever he moved. His tie clip was also a key. What he needed with all of those keys was anyone's guess.

The scribe blotted the page. At last the paper was folded lengthwise, and twice horizontally, and one end was tucked into the other. Monica was asked to stand with Leonard opposite her.

"Cup your hands," Rabbi Shemkin instructed her. "And you," he said to Leonard, "repeat after me: 'And now I do release, discharge, and divorce you to be on your own, so that you are permitted and have authority over yourself to go and marry any man you desire.'"

Noa held her breath. Next to her, Rachel sniffed.

"'No person may object against you from this day onward, and you are permitted to every man.'"

She thought she heard Leonard's voice quiver with "every man," but wasn't sure. Turning to Rachel, she saw the young rabbi with the blond beard staring at her, and only slowly did he avert his blue eyes.

"'This shall be for you from me a bill of dismissal,'" Rabbi Shemkin continued, "'a letter of release, and a document of absolution, in accordance with the law of Moses and Israel,'" and Leonard repeated that, too, now full-throated. He was difficult and commanding, it was true. His injuries were such that, just when it was most needed, he failed to see beyond his anger or pain to that of others. Once upon a time it had charmed Monica that Leonard darned his own socks. In one of the stories they'd liked to tell, Monica woke in his bachelor apartment to find Leonard bent over the sock, sucking on the ends of the thread as his mother had taught him to do. But over time Monica stopped being able to see the light that came through this small break in the stubborn monotony of character.

Following the rabbi's instruction, Leonard laid the rectangle on top of Monica's cupped hands. It was too big to fit into her palms, and reflexively she clamped her thumbs down so it wouldn't slip.

"No!" the rabbis all shouted together.

Apparently the wife wasn't allowed to move her hands to take the paper: it had to be given. The barbarity of the whole thing seemed not to bother Monica. Perhaps it seemed to her a fitting end to the rest of her wrongheaded marriage. She seemed to Noa already not there. Though where her mother had been, always, was a place that she, too, had found unreachable. Leonard gave it again, and this time Monica held her hands very still, as if she were receiving a stunned bird. Then she was made to hold the paper high over her head. Monica's arms shot straight up, the hands clutched around the paper folded according to some ancient Jewish origami.

After it was over, they drove to the Italian place Leonard and Monica liked. Leonard's opera albums filled the CD changer in the trunk; Pavarotti flowed forth. Noa had one more year left of school, and over their salads Leonard and Monica told her that in the fall they would take turns living in the house with her until she graduated. This was a nebulous plan, it being only May. As for the summer, they gave Noa the choice of going to Megiddo with Leonard, or Vienna with Monica. She protested: last year she had spent her summer working at a florist shop, and she planned to do the same again. She was saving money to travel to Brazil, Peru, Argentina, maybe as far as Easter Island, after she graduated from high school. Why should she have to change her plans just because her parents had decided to upend their lives? She would be bored in Megiddo, and claustrophobic in her grandmother's apartment crowded with heavy furniture, the silk curtains permanently closed to keep out the sun. An argument ensued, but Noa stood her ground. She would be perfectly fine on her own, she insisted. Rachel wasn't listening, busy texting her boyfriend in Boston. In Rachel's features,

Leonard and Monica had found an early harmony, unlike in Noa's, where, after puberty, Leonard had prevailed. She'd also inherited Leonard's height, which made it easy for her parents to see her as older than she was. Besides, practical as they were, Leonard and Monica had always believed in treating their children like adults. So why make a show of treating her like a child now? She dug in until her parents gave up. If they felt guilty about the divorce, or following the course of their own desires, they hadn't sustained it for long. Leonard left for Israel in mid-June, and Monica a week later. Jack and Roberta Berkowitz, her parents' oldest friends, were enlisted to check on her, which Roberta did, calling from the aisles of Whole Foods to see if Noa wanted to come for dinner, or if there was anything that she needed. But there never was.

IN THE KITCHEN, Noa boiled water for coffee. The only remaining full-time occupant of a house that would be sold in a year, she rearranged things as she saw fit. The Sumerian fertility jug that her parents had bought together the year they'd met, she put in the hall closet behind Leonard's tennis rackets. Fat and earthy, it had a foreboding air. She also took down the photos from the fridge. Rachel and Noa, Leonard and Monica, smiling glibly at the top of a mountain, or in the golden light of the desert, now possessed a false quality. The whole house, it seemed, had been organized around principles that were no longer true, and now these arrangements seemed disingenuous. Maybe that was why Noa had stopped sleeping in her bedroom after her parents left, and taken to sleeping on the sofa instead. This had bothered Gabe. He didn't like having the poster of

Goya's old man staring down on his nudity. He called him Old Egghead, and blamed him for ruining things. But two weeks earlier they had broken up, and she left Old Egghead on the wall. Lying on the sofa under his purview, Noa could see the dining room table where her family had always celebrated Passover, Thanksgiving, birthdays, and other special occasions, accompanied by friends and family. Her cousins called her uncle and aunt Daddy and Mommy, something she had sometimes envied. But close as she was with her own parents, those two words possessed a kind of intimacy, a silliness even, that didn't fit Leonard and Monica, and would have made her embarrassed to utter. One summer at the kibbutz when she was seven or eight, Noa had taken to calling her father Abba, but when they returned home at the end of August the name had been left behind with the other toys, stones, and knickknacks they had collected over the summer, which could not fit into the suitcase, or would not be needed back home.

While she was eating her cereal, Noa's cell phone rang. It was Leonard, who had been following the news: more than a hundred thousand acres already, the fire crews pushed beyond exhaustion, no sign of containment. Strong winds had carried the embers into the city, and thousands had been forced to evacuate. He'd already called the Berkowitzes; Jack would come to get her. But Noa wouldn't agree to it. She was in no danger, she argued. The fires were far enough away. To change the subject, she asked how things were going at the dig. Worked up about the lab results of some burned bricks, Leonard eagerly launched into a description of the newest developments. The tests had revealed that the formation the bricks had been found in was not original; that they had been reused after an older city had been destroyed. When bricks are burned, their magnetic north at the time of the fire is preserved forever. This is a fact she had known since she was young, but now she let her father go on about it while she drank the milk left in her cereal bowl, washed the bowl, and set it to dry upside down on the rack. Having pulled the carpet out from under the existing paradigm of tenth-century archaeology, as he liked to say, Leonard was now trying to get to the bottom of the question of who had destroyed the late Iron Age city. Noa had meant to tell him about the call from the rabbi, but before she could, Leonard was called away by his second- or third-in-command, his expertise required. He would call her back later, he said, and they would discuss then what would be most prudent.

Seeing the time, Noa realized she was late for work. She sniffed the armpits of a shirt lying on the floor next to the sofa, and pulled it over her head without bothering with the buttons or a bra. Her chest had been flat until she was fourteen, and then she'd developed two small mounds, as if her body would agree only grudgingly to womanhood. Monica had insisted on taking her to buy bras, though she'd hardly required them.

She liked the tropical climate of the florist shop, and its sense of perpetual event. Something was always happening to someone, some fact of life, happy or sad, that called for commemoration. The day before, they'd had to make twenty-five centerpieces for a wedding. The ranunculus had arrived shut up in themselves and had to be coaxed open with warm water. She'd stripped the fringed leaves off the lower stems and arranged the flowers in silver bowls. The bride had wanted lilac, but the shipment was delayed because of the fires. Insulated by many layers of people doing her bidding, the bride was dealing with this disappointment, though her bridesmaid kept calling to report her displeasure.

Noa found the car keys in the pocket of yesterday's shorts and headed outside. There had been a heat wave for over a week and the car was a furnace, but she didn't have time to wait for it to cool, and threw an old towel down on the seat so that it wouldn't burn the back of her thighs. Old Mr. Frankel, the neighbor, was standing on his dry front lawn in a rumpled robe. The Frankels' house was a replica of theirs, having been built by the same developer. When Noa was little, Mrs. Frankel would sometimes invite her in and give her cookies in her dining room, which was the same as their dining room, only filled with glass furniture and her collection of kitsch Judaica. Mrs. Frankel was from Queens, and was as much of the new world as Mr. Frankel was of the old, having fled Europe with his parents during the war. Dark photographs of Mr. Frankel's dead hung in the hall that led to the bathroom. But slowly, over the years, the stand of bamboo that bordered their backyards had grown so thick that there was no longer any passage through, and Noa grew older and stopped visiting. Occasionally Leonard would go over to fix something for the Frankels, or sort out a bank letter Mr. Frankel didn't understand. A few months ago Mrs. Frankel had had a stroke in her sleep and died. Leonard, Monica, and Noa had walked over for the shiva, and as they stepped inside the Frankels' house, its long-forgotten smell came back to her. Later, Leonard told them that Mr. Frankel had taken him aside. Alone in the bedroom where two nights earlier his wife had passed away, he'd told Leonard that he'd buried something in the garden and needed to dig it up. At first Mr. Frankel had not wanted to reveal what needed exhuming, but when he saw that he would not be able to engage Leonard's expertise without divulging the truth, he opened the top drawer of a dresser and handed him a carefully folded receipt. It was for a hundred and fifty gold Krugerrands, purchased in 1973. For more than forty years the coins had lain at the bottom of the garden, sealed in two Maxwell coffee cans and wrapped in Saran. Only he had forgotten precisely where. But why? Leonard had asked. Why had he buried them in the first place? Mr. Frankel had thrown up his sun-spotted hands. "In case" was all he would say, and nothing more. Now Noa wondered whether Leonard had ever helped Mr. Frankel to locate the gold. She would have liked to stop to ask Mr. Frankel, but she was already late.

She'd driven to the end of the street before remembering the rabbi, and paused with her hand on the gearshift, deliberating. Then she reversed back down the street, jogged back into the kitchen, and came out again with the envelope from the State Supreme Court. Clutching it to her chest, Noa called to Mr. Frankel, who was looking up at the bright sky. Noa looked up, too, and saw a helicopter hanging above, churning the smoggy air.

AT THE SHOP they were already loading the centerpieces into the van. The bride didn't care about the immense, untamed fires, the acres of trees burning, the homes destroyed, or the two firefighters who had already lost their lives to the blaze: the wedding would proceed no matter what. "Come hell or high water," the father of the bride had said, however unfitting the expression was for the natural disaster at hand, and threatened to sue if the centerpieces didn't arrive. But his firm was an important client of the small florist shop, and so the owner insisted that every effort be made to get the arrangements of ranunculus—which were not even lilac, and so already cause for offense—to the house where the wedding would take place.

Noa's boss called out to her from behind a curtain of fronds.

"The highway is blocked off, and Bobbi isn't here yet. I need you to go with Nick to deliver."

She helped him load the centerpieces into the van. There were twenty-five altogether, plus three large bouquets in urns, and the bridal bouquet. As she set down the last centerpiece in the cool interior of the van, her phone buzzed against her hip. It was her mother, and she let it ring. But Monica was persistent and didn't let up.

"I'm at work!"

"Why work? Leonard said you were going to the Berkowitzes'!"

Noa clamped the phone to her ear with her shoulder and began hooking up the bungee cords to hold the vases in place. "I haven't spoken to the Berkowitzes. We have a wedding."

"What wedding? Who's getting married at a time like this?"

"Delivering now. I have to go."

"I've been watching online all morning. It says the fires—"

Noa slammed the back doors of the van and went around to the passenger seat as Nick started the engine.

"I really have to call you back," she insisted, cutting her mother off.

"This is serious, Noa. You shouldn't be driving around the city at a time like this. It isn't safe."

"It's fine. The roads are open here, the fires are miles away. I'll call you later. Say hi to Grandma."

"She doesn't remember you. Yesterday she thought I was her mother."

Noa felt a stab of hurt. She didn't say what she wanted to: that the whole family was disintegrating. Instead she said a firm goodbye and returned the phone to her pocket. She slid her feet out of her sandals and pressed her toes into the dash. The palm trees outside were thrashing in the wind. She thought how if her grandmother had been present enough to receive the news of Monica and Leonard's divorce, she would have been shocked and outraged. She would have been capable of any number of outsize reactions, but none would have been accepting. Maybe Monica had waited until her mother was sheltered by dementia so as to spare them both. Or maybe it had been her grandmother's frailty, the fact of her approaching death, that made Monica feel how time was running out for the things she still wanted from life. Or had the whole thing been Leonard's idea? Her parents had presented a united front, making it impossible for their daughters to know who had instigated the separation. No one was hurt; each had gotten what they wanted. They were in agreement about no longer needing to agree on how to live the rest of their lives.

On the news, the reports of the fire's progress kept coming, the facts circled over and repeated. The tons of water and fire retardants released from the air, the efforts to box it inside a buffer zone, the crews working in lines, hacking away at whatever could burn. The van left the coastal roads, and the airconditioning momentarily brought in the smell of smoke. Nick switched off the radio. This was his last month of work; he was moving north at the end of July. He told Noa about the yurt he'd been constructing on his friend's land. It would be different to live in the round, without corners, he said. With his free hand he scrolled on his phone to a photo of the view from the property of distant blue mountains. He was studying biodynamic farming. The land was a cooperative, united in the goal of sustainability and community. In the summer, they swam naked in the Yuba River. He showed her a photo of the passionate river, rushing wild and muddy after a storm. Now it would already be green, he said, pouring down from the High Sierra, clear all the way to the granite bottom.

Nick probably didn't believe in marriage, Noa decided as they made their way toward the bride's house in the hills. He probably didn't even believe in monogamy, considering it a convention as obsolete as corners. Did Monica and Leonard no longer believe in monogamy, either? And what about her? What did she believe in? She thought of Gabe, and with an ache of longing his body came back to her, the way it smelled, and how his stomach went concave when she slid her fingers beneath the elastic of his underwear. His face when he came. By now some other girl must have seen that expression, the one that looked like both pleasure and pain. The girl at the pool where he was a lifeguard, maybe, with shiny hair and breasts that sat like per-fect oranges in her bikini top, who wouldn't hesitate to sleep with him. Noa imagined Gabe's mouth on hers, and her longing opened into jealousy and pain. Feeling her face flush, she turned to look out the window.

AT THE BRIDE's house, the pool man was skimming the purple jacaranda flowers out of the water with his long net. A white tent with gauzy sides had been erected to shade the guests from the sun and wind, and the sound of a hammer rang out from within. The wedding organizer came to meet them and led them along a path edged with lavender. Noa broke off a flower and crushed it between her fingers. The smell it released reminded her of Israel, of the stucco houses of the kibbutz, with their gardens decorated with old tractor parts used as planters, out of which spilled succulents in all shapes and sizes. Inside the tent, twenty-four round tables were covered with white tablecloths, and a raised dais was being constructed for the table of the bride and groom.

While they carried the flower arrangements in from the van, the bride's mother came out of the house and called out to the wedding planner, who didn't hear her, busy giving instructions over the phone. The mother of the bride wore high heels that clicked anxiously across the wooden dance floor. She stopped to examine the flowers Noa had just set down. As she fingered the petals, her fallen face fell further. Her front teeth were stained with lipstick. The arrangements were too small, she said. They had expected lilac. Her daughter would not be happy.

Noa looked down and again felt the heat rising at the back

of her neck. Who did these people think they were? To shout about flowers? To celebrate while a few miles away people were losing their homes and dying in the brutal fight against the fires? She felt that if she answered now, she might not be able to control what came out, and so she called Nick and retreated to the van.

Inside the cool interior, she closed her eyes and exhaled. Her anger had been at a constant low boil for months, always ready to spill over. Before they'd broken up, she'd started fights with Gabe over nothing, overreacting to the smallest things. She wanted to be left alone, and then once he was gone, she was furious at him for leaving. Or she would curl into him like a child, but when he'd utter some offhand comment that rubbed her the wrong way, she'd turn away, cold and injured, and even when she wanted to reach for him again, she couldn't. She hadn't agreed to have sex with him. He'd done it before, and she had never, and this imbalance bothered her. It wasn't that she was romantic about her first time. More that she was too aware of how the moment would be differently valued in each of their lives, not just then but always. The other girl, his first, would be remembered after Noa might long be forgotten, whereas she would be promising to remember him forever. "Make up your mind!" he shouted at her before they broke up, when once again she'd gone from warm to cold, and given him her back. But aside from whether or not to sleep with him, what had been up to her, really? He was leaving for college in August. He would find someone else, a girl more easygoing than her, lighthearted and beautiful. She told him as much, and when he protested, she insisted, calmly, practically, as if she were invulnerable.

Had she always been this way? Her independence was a matter of pride. Monica and Leonard claimed she'd been like that since she was a baby. One of the earliest stories they told about her was how, when she was only two, she had walked into the first day of preschool without looking back. She'd climbed onto the rocking horse and screamed when any of the other children wanted a turn. She'd sat astride the horse, stubborn and imperious, and used her lung power to keep the others at bay. Noa had never really questioned this telling of the story, how it had come to be used, like all of the earliest stories parents tell children about themselves, as proof of character. But why hadn't she hung back and clung to her mother? Mustn't there have been a need for independence long before it became the story about her, and a point of pride? Wasn't the pride only vulnerability masquerading as strength, until at last it had become one? But as with all strengths that grew out of need, its foundation had never been solid. It was built on top of a hole. Wouldn't she have held tight to her mother if Monica had been a mother she could reliably cling to, rather than the comfort of a rocking horse?

Nick came back and reported that the owner of the shop was on her way with a supply of flowers to redo the bouquets. They waited inside the van with the air-conditioning on full blast. When Noa's phone rang again, it was Leonard, and she let it ring through to voice mail. She imagined him where he was, standing on the tell at dusk. The hill beneath his feet had been man-made by slow accumulation: layers of life and its destruction, continuous from 7000 BC to biblical times. The jewel in the crown of biblical archaeology! as he never let anyone forget.

No other site in Israel possessed more Bronze or Iron Age monuments, he told the students at the start of every summer. As he looked south across the Jezreel Valley, his eyes would come to rest on the distant blue hills of Samaria, and the view produced a flicker of agitation: to think of the wealth of secrets buried there, off-limits, not to be touched in his lifetime! From atop the tell, Leonard left her a message. She didn't need to listen to it to know what it said. But she was not going to the Berkowitzes'.

Nick took out rolling papers and a tin box of weed. He pinched up a clump, worked it between his fingers, and sprinkled the fragrant grass into the fold of the paper. She didn't usually like getting high, but she was bored and annoyed enough to take a few hits. The smoke burned her throat, but soon her chest relaxed and lightness filled her head.

When she had to go to the bathroom, she got out of the van and headed toward the house. The enormous front door was propped open, and the catering staff sailed hurriedly in and out. She stopped one with a box of Beaujolais on his shoulder and asked for directions to the bathroom. "Ask in the kitchen," he said, gesturing toward the interior.

It was dark and cool there. Through the leaded-glass windows of the library, the garden was a blur of muted greens. She made her way down the oak-paneled corridor, everything at a greater remove than usual. Trying the first door she came to, she discovered a closet full of golf clubs. Soon she came to the kitchen, which was bustling with activity. Three chefs in white paper hats and checked pants were giving orders to the rest of the staff. No one even glanced at her; they were cooking for two hundred and fifty. Noa continued down the hall until she came to a wide-carpeted staircase. The need to pee was now urgent, and, emboldened by the weed, she went up.

An antique console with a rounded belly and claw feet guarded the landing. On its marble top, photos were displayed of a girl at nine, twelve, sixteen. A little farther on was a doorway, and through it Noa glimpsed the gleaming brass of a faucet. She hurried in, locked the door behind her, and sank with relief onto the toilet, kicking off her sandals. She sat there for a while, relaxing in peace. Through the wall she heard laughter, though it might have been crying. If she ever married, she would elope, she decided. Or have the wedding at a dive, someplace that didn't suggest any expectation. It seemed only to be asking for trouble, a wedding like this.

Someone jiggled the door handle. Noa stood and turned on the tap. "One minute," she called, quickly drying her hands on the soft terry cloth towel and opening the door. It was the girl in the photos, standing with her bridal dress gathered around her torso. She was older, but still young, with a face that was somehow monkeylike and yet not unpretty. She didn't look much older than twenty-two or -three.

"Oh," she said, surprised. "Who are you?"

"I'm with the caterer," Noa lied.

The bride hesitated a moment, but as everyone in the house was under her command, she gave it no further thought and turned around, lifting the wavy tendrils curled that morning by an iron.

"Can you zip this?"

Noa wiped her hands again on her shorts and took up the tiny zipper. The fabric strained at the seams as she tried to zip it up. She thought it might rip, but finally the zipper pull passed the widest point of the bride's broad back and slid smoothly to the top.

"I was a swimmer," she explained, turning to face Noa. To prove the point, her lashes were wet, as if the swimmer-bride had just surfaced from underwater. Or maybe it had been crying Noa had heard through the wall after all.

"Come here, I need help with something else."

Noa didn't liked being ordered around, but she couldn't resist her curiosity. She followed the bride into the bedroom. It was decorated with her first- and second-prize ribbons, for not only swim competitions but equestrian ones as well. Pictures of horses were framed on the wall like beloved relatives. Above the desk, a collection of Hello Kitty erasers and pencil sharpeners were displayed on the glass shelves. Noa had once had some like that; she'd forgotten all about them, and seeing them brought back the strong sensation of her childhood. Impulsively, just as she had sometimes done as a child, she stuck out her hand and picked up an eraser, and just before the bride turned back to her, she slipped it into her pocket.

"I can't walk in these," the bride said, gesturing to her high-heeled silver shoes.

It was true that she looked ungainly, stomping down hard on her toes. Noa wondered where her bridesmaids had gone, or whoever was supposed to be guiding her on the last, risky stretch of a path that might still be abandoned, where doubt and bewilderment lay in wait to ambush her. In Jewish weddings, the *kalla*, the bride, was meant to be treated like a queen, tended to like royalty, an approach that, however ancient, was filled with wisdom of human psychology, of the frailty of the heart. The frailty of the heart, and the shame of the body, because the Orthodox brides had never been with a man, nor their grooms with a woman, a circumstance they were obligated to reverse directly after the ceremonies. And so perhaps the royal treatment was designed to distract from any lurking terror, too.

The bride's pale forehead wrinkled.

"I'll fall on my face if I wear these, I swear."

Noa felt a flicker of agitation that the bride did not see the absurdity of the whole situation, not even a little. Seeing a pair of old canvas sneakers kicked off at the foot of the bed, she pointed.

"How about those?"

The bride began to laugh. Her eyes were shining. She gave the impression of being vaguely crazy. She kicked her feet free of the high heels, hitched up her train, and, restored to her natural agility, leaped across the room. Her muscular body, trained to swim leagues and exert dominion over horses, to win and never to lose, gave the impression of knowing itself better than her mind. She slipped her feet into the sneakers without bothering with the laces, and danced over to the mirrored closets. But as she surveyed her reflection, the laugh disappeared from her twisted mouth.

A long silence passed. Then the bride met Noa's eyes in the mirror.

"You're not with the caterer," she said darkly.

Noa said nothing.

"I can tell from the dirt under your nails."

It was true: the moons under her fingernails were black. It was like that all summer, the potting soil washed clean only when she swam.

Noa shrugged, unbothered by being caught out in a lie. An inner sense of her own abundant reason often led her to see others as lacking in the same, a quality she had inherited from Leonard, and which Gabe had often pointed out was a form of superiority. But wasn't everyone convinced of their own unimpeachable reason? Not everyone, Gabe had said; most leave open the possibility that they might be wrong, and at the very least that other ways of thinking are not lunacy. Noa accepted his point, if only to demonstrate her openness to other people's thinking. This, too, was not original to her: Leonard, when accused of obstinacy, could be magnanimous for the rest of the day, until he forgot and became himself again.

"I didn't want to raise your fury about the flowers. Your mother said you wouldn't like the bouquets. There's no lilac, and they're too small and need to be redone. We're waiting for the owner to deliver more flowers."

"My mother," the bride groaned, as if she'd just been reminded of bad news. But she didn't say more, and, called back to the task at hand, lifted a mass of gauzy material from where it lay on her bed and handed it to Noa. The veil was attached to a tortoiseshell comb, and the bride turned her back again, this time so that Noa could see where to slide it into the coiffed hair, half gathered up with bobby pins. It was stiff from spray, and Noa had to push hard to work the teeth of the comb into the mass. Finally it was secure, and the bride turned back around and lowered her chin solemnly, waiting for the veil to be lifted over her face. Taken by the power of the ritual, she closed her eyes. Her features turned soft and vague as they disappeared behind the lace, and Noa felt a shiver, too, as if she really were to be the last to look upon the bride's face as it was then, before whatever was to happen—the undertaking of grave responsibility, the induction into secret wisdom—that would change it afterward. Slowly the bride turned to look at herself in the mirror, and Noa turned, too, surprised at her own reflection, tall and lanky, with flat chest and dirt under her nails, suddenly boyish, as if all her femininity had been stolen by the bride in virginal white lace.

But there was no time to study the changes in themselves further, because the voice of the bride's mother, shrill with the anxiety of imperfection, or still deeper than that, of losing her only child to loyalties greater than the one to her, rang out from the bottom of the stairs. Their eyes met in the mirror, and much passed between them in that moment that Noa didn't fully understand. She offered a mumbled good-luck to the bride, and hurried out of the bedroom, hiding out in the bathroom until the mother of the bride had passed before making her way downstairs again and out to the van.

BY THE TIME they got back to the florist shop, it was already three o'clock, but there was more work to do. The fires hadn't put much of a pause to the passion, longing, grief, or simple desire to mark anniversaries, it seemed, all of which called for flowers. Short of staff, Noa's boss, Ciara, asked her to stay on until all the orders were complete at well past seven. The radio spilled news of the fires nonstop: two more firemen had lost their lives, and hundreds more homes had been evacuated. Ciara, who years ago had lost a son to brain cancer and was used to variance between her private life and the celebrations of others, worked silently alongside her at the cutting table. When Noa had finished the last bouquet, a tropical affair with fronds and gaudy birds of paradise, she rinsed her hands in the enormous metal sink. Scrubbing her nails, she thought of the bride, who must already have been married by now.

Only when she got into her car did she see the envelope from the Supreme Court lying on the passenger seat, and remember her promise to the rabbi. She was exhausted, and the sadness that had been welling in her chest now begged to be relieved by the familiar smell of home, where she could collapse on the sofa and watch TV. But the rabbi was leaving for Poland tomorrow, and without the necessary paperwork, nothing would be final. He had wanted everything to be in order: the disorder of what had been broken and upended, annulled and canceled, transformed magically into order by the simple filing of the paperwork in the official archives of the Jewish court. And though Noa had no desire to aid and abet this granting of order to what she knew would long remain, might always remain, a disorder in her heart, she also did not wish to be the one to stand in its way. She entered the address the rabbi had given her into her phone, ignoring the missed calls and texts that had come from her parents earlier in the day. She had repeated her decision, and eventually they'd had to accept it. Being late where they were, and the fires no closer, each must have gone off to sleep, since her phone had been quiet for hours. Now she saw that the address, in an unfamiliar neighborhood, was only twenty minutes away, not far from the synagogue where the rabbi had performed—if *performed* was the right word—the get. And though she knew it might take longer if the closure of roads had caused more traffic than predicted, she turned the wheel in the direction the GPS instructed.

IT WAS A neighborhood of modest houses set back from front lawns unadorned by flowers. In the dusk, the Hasids went past at a tilt in dark suits, in denial of the heat, the women in long skirts and sleeves pushing and lugging children, bent and hurrying. Always hurrying, these people—it was Leonard's voice she heard in her head. Hurrying to get one last mitzvah under the belt, though the Messiah himself, that great scorekeeper of Jewish action, Jewish fate, was in no hurry himself.

The rabbi's house was as nondescript as the rest, aside from an aluminum frame chair left out under a tree, the nylon straps of the seat sagging deeply, as if someone had sat many hours thinking there. But when Noa parked and crossed the lawn at a diagonal on the way to the front door, she saw that the patchy grass around the chair was littered with cigarette butts, the chair merely the seat of a bad habit the rabbi's wife wouldn't condone in the house.

With Leonard and Monica's divorce papers under her arm, she rang the bell. But when the door opened, it wasn't the rabbi's wife, but the young assistant with the sparse blond beard. His face brightened with surprise when he saw her. She asked if the rabbi was home, holding up the envelope by way of explanation. No, the young rabbi said, the whole family was at a wedding. "Seems everyone is getting married today," Noa said.

The young rabbi raised his eyebrows and smiled. She clutched the envelope, not yet ready to give it up. Did she want to come in? he asked.

Noa wondered if he had even heard about the fires, which couldn't be smelled from there. A bowl of fruit, pears and purple grapes, their skin ripe and frosted, was set out on the kitchen table. Sit down, he offered, gesturing to a chair. He boiled water in the kettle for tea, and brought her some in a glass. She sipped it, grateful for his simple act of kindness. Watching the familiar ease with which he moved around the kitchen, it occurred to her that this was not merely an assistant but the rabbi's son. He sat down opposite her and stirred a spoonful of sugar into his own glass, his lips moving in silent blessing before he drank.

"Noa, right?" he said.

She couldn't remember introducing herself by name on the day of the get, but he must have heard her parents or sister address her.

"I'm Aviel, but everyone calls me Avi."

Noa looked hungrily at the fruit, and Avi, sensitive and alert, pushed the bowl toward her.

"Please, take," he said, and got up to bring her a plate and knife. She thought of the Hasids who sometimes stood on street corners, stopping passersby to ask if they were Jewish, and if they wanted Shabbat candles, or to put on tefillin, and wondered if Avi's hospitality was merely practical, born of the Rebbe's command to draw in wayward Jews, to bring them into the fold where they, too, could add to the count of mitzvot that would hasten the coming of the Moshiach.

"How are your parents?" he asked. He didn't know them, but

had been present at an intimate moment of their lives, which made him something other than a stranger.

"They're away," Noa offered. "Leonard is an archaeologist, and every summer he goes back to Israel to lead an excavation. And Monica is in Vienna, taking care of my grandmother."

"And you stayed behind?"

Cutting a pear, Noa told him about her job at the florist shop, and how she was saving money to travel next summer. She had been many places with her parents, but never to South America. If she got as far as Chile and still had enough money, she would make the journey to Easter Island, to see the monolithic heads carved in volcanic stone that had fascinated her since she first saw photographs of their strange faces as a child. For a long time no one knew how their primitive makers had transported them from the quarry to the coast, where they were mounted on massive platforms, their faces turned inland. When Leonard told her, a few years later, that researchers had finally figured out how it was done, she was disappointed and didn't want to know, preferring to preserve the mystery. It was a difference between her and Leonard, who had spent his life digging to the bottom of things. And Monica, too, a professor of comparative literature whose effort to squeeze the meaning out of German and Hebrew texts was exhaustive. It worried Noa that she couldn't yet think of any profession that appealed to her in which this holding on to mystery had any value.

Avi listened with fascination, as if he were imagining her traveling alone on buses barreling through the jungle, around dangerous curving mountain passes, toward the mysteries of childhood. He, too, liked to travel, and had recently returned after two years of running the Chabad house in Bangkok. That he had seen the wider world might explain the knowingness Noa sensed in his face. She remembered how she had caught him looking at her during the get, and now she saw again that there was a flickering brightness in his eyes, a curiosity at odds with the conformity of his dark suit. The cigarette butts by the lawn chair must have been his, not the elder rabbi's, a habit he might have picked up in Thailand. What place did curiosity have, Noa wondered, in a world like his?

"And what about you? Why'd you stay behind instead of going to the wedding with everyone else?"

"There's no shortage of weddings. My mother is one of eight sisters and brothers. I have a cousin getting married nearly every month."

She thought she should relinquish the envelope and go, but something kept her. Avi's fingers rested on his empty tea glass, long and delicate. She saw him look at her bare legs, and the knowledge that such nakedness had never before been glimpsed in that kitchen gave her a sudden sense of power.

"And you? When are you getting married?"

The sky was darkening outside the window.

"Next year, *im yirtzeh HaShem*."

They went on talking. He asked her about Leonard's work in Israel, and she told him about Tel Megiddo, formed by the remains of twenty-five civilizations that rose and fell, destroyed by earthquake or fire, until the next was rebuilt atop the ruins. How for twenty years Leonard had been uncovering these layers of destruction, destroying them in turn in order to discover the truths about the people who lived and died there. How?

Avi asked, fascinated, and she described the slow and method-
ical work, the baskets of shards collected and sorted each day,
the carbon-14 used to determine when a living thing, a seed or
grain left in a cup, had ceased to live. As she spoke, she sensed in
him the familiar shiver of wonder and fear she'd sometimes been
struck with as a child, looking around her from the vantage of a
distant future, and wondering what would be left to piece back
together the rituals of vanished belief, vanished hopes and hun-
gers, to solve the mystery of why she and all those near to her
had passed out of existence.

He waited for her to say more, but she had run out of the
words for things. Finally she put her fingers on the edge of the
envelope that contained the judgment of divorce, then slid it
across the table. Far away, her parents were getting on with their
lives. Avi took it and held it for a moment in his delicate hands,
then put it on the counter where the rabbi would find it. Noa
stood up as if to go, but even as she stood she knew, from the
depths of her body, that she wasn't going. She remained standing, swaying on her feet. Avi watched her, full of amazement. At
last she stepped toward him, and it seemed that her fingers were
reaching for a very long time until at last they touched the blond
hairs of his cheek. He closed his eyes, his lips moving. Gently,
she covered them with her own, as if to still them, but instead
she took into herself whatever they were saying in that ancient
language, and felt the desire grow live in her groin. His eyes
were open now, and moving her mouth away, she unbuttoned
her shirt. It wasn't much, but she felt it was a gift all the same,
and took his trembling fingers and put them on her breast. His
thumb moved over her nipple, and she held her breath and shiv-

ered. She undid her shorts and let them fall to the floor, and was about to step out of her underwear when he turned to the window in fear, as if someone outside might see into the wonders of what was happening within. As if the fires were nearly upon them, burning closer and closer, as uncontainable as all fires that sweep away the old order to make way for the next. He clutched her hand in his sweaty hand, and led her through the dark living room to his small bedroom at the back of the house. And there, in the narrow twin bed, she gave to him what she wanted to give, and took from him what she needed, and when the splitting pain shot through her, she bit into his shoulder to stifle her cry, and had no words for the blessing.

Seeing Ershadi

I'd been in the company for over a year by then. It had been my dream to dance for the choreographer since I first saw his work, and for a decade all of my desire had been focused on getting there. I'd sacrificed whatever was necessary during the years of rigorous training. When at last I auditioned and he invited me to join his company, I dropped everything and flew to Tel Aviv. We rehearsed from noon until five, and I devoted myself to the choreographer's process and vision without reserve, applied myself without reserve. Sometimes tears came spontaneously, from something that had rushed upward and burst. When I met people in the bars and cafés, I spoke excitedly about the experience of working with the choreographer, and told them that I felt I was on the verge of constant discovery. Until one day I realized that I had become fanatical. That what I had taken to be devotion had crossed the line into something else. And though my awareness of this was a dark blot on what had been, until then, a pure joy, I didn't know what to do with it.

Exhausted after rehearsal, I'd either walk to the sea or go home to watch a film until it got late enough to go out and meet people. I couldn't go to the beach as often as I'd have liked because the choreographer said he wanted the skin all over our bodies to be as pale as the skin on our asses. I'd developed tendinitis in my ankle, which made it necessary for me to ice it after dancing, and so I found myself watching a lot of films, lying on my back with my foot up. I saw everything with Jean-Louis Trintignant until he got so old that his imminent death began to be too depressing, and then I switched to Louis Garrel, who is beautiful enough to live forever. Sometimes, when my friend Romi wasn't working, she came to watch with me. By the time I finished with Garrel it was winter, and swimming was out of the question anyway, so I spent two weeks inside with Ingmar Bergman. With the New Year, I resolved to give up Bergman and the weed I smoked every night, and because the title was appealing, and it was made far from Sweden, I downloaded *Taste of Cherry*, by the Iranian director Abbas Kiarostami.

It opens with the actor Homayoun Ershadi's face. He plays Mr. Badii, a middle-aged man driving slowly through the streets of Tehran in search of someone, scanning crowds of men clamoring to be hired for labor. Not finding what he's looking for, he drives on into the arid hills outside the city. When he sees a man on the side of the road, he slows the car and offers him a ride; the man refuses, and when Badii continues to try to convince him, the man gets angry and stalks off, looking back darkly over his shoulder. After more driving, five or seven minutes of it—an eternity in a film—a young soldier appears, hitchhiking, on the side of the road, and Badii offers him a ride to his barracks. He begins to question the boy about his life as a soldier and his family in Kurdistan, and the more personal and direct the questions, the more awkward the situation becomes for the soldier, who is soon squirming in his seat. Some twenty minutes into the film, Badii finally comes out with it: he's searching for someone to bury him. He's dug his own grave into the side of one of those bone-dry hills, and tonight he plans to take pills and lie down in it; all he needs is for someone to come in the morning to check that he's really dead, and then to cover him with twenty shovelfuls of earth.

The soldier opens the car door, leaps out, and flees into the hills. What Mr. Badii is asking amounts to being an accomplice to a crime, since suicide is forbidden in the Quran. The camera gazes after the soldier as he grows smaller and smaller until he disappears altogether into the landscape, then it returns to Ershadi's extraordinary face, a face that remains almost completely expressionless throughout the film, and yet manages to convey a gravity and depth of feeling that could never come from acting—that could only come of an intimate knowledge of what it is to be pushed to the brink of hopelessness. Not once in the film are we told anything about the life of Mr. Badii, or what might have brought him to decide to end it. Nor do we witness his despair. Everything we know about the depth contained within him we get from his expressionless face, which also tells us about the depth contained within the actor Homayoun Ershadi, about whose life we know even less. When I did a search, I discovered that Ershadi was an architect with no training or experience as an actor when Kiarostami saw him sitting in his car in traffic, lost in thought, and knocked on his window. And it was easy to understand, just looking at his face: how the world seemed to bend toward Ershadi, as if it needed him more than he needed it.

His face did something to me. Or rather the film, with its compassion and its utterly jarring ending, which I won't give away, did something to me. But then again, you could also say that in some sense the film was only his face: his face and those lonely hills.

NOT LONG AFTER that, it became warm again. When I opened the windows the smell of cats came in, but also of sunshine, salt, and oranges. Along the wide streets, the ficus trees showed new green. I wanted to take something from this renewal, to be a small part of it, but the truth was that my body was increasingly run-down. My ankle was only getting worse the more I danced on it, and I was going through a bottle of Advil a week. When it was time for the company to go on tour again, I didn't feel like going, even though it was to Japan, where I'd always wanted to travel. I wanted to stay and rest and feel the sun, I wanted to lie on the beach with Romi and smoke and talk about boys, but I packed my bag and rode with a couple of the other dancers to the airport.

We had three performances in Tokyo, followed by two free days, and a group of us decided to go to Kyoto. It was still winter in Japan. On the train from Tokyo, the heavy tile roofs went by, houses with small windows. We found a *ryokan* to stay at, with a room done up with tatami mats and shoji panels, and walls the color and texture of sand. Everything struck me as in-comprehensible; I constantly made mistakes. I wore the special bathroom slippers out of the bathroom and across the room. When I asked the woman who served us an elaborate dinner what happened if something was spilled on the tatami mat, she began to scream with laughter. If she could have fallen off her seat, she would have. But the room had no seats at all. Instead, she stuffed the wrapping for my hot towel into the gaping sleeve of her kimono, but very beautifully, so that one could forget the fact that she was disposing of garbage.

On the last morning I got up early and went out with a map, on which I had marked the temples I wanted to visit. Everything was still stripped and bare. Not even the plum trees were in blossom yet, so there was nothing to bring out the hordes with their cameras, and I'd gotten used to being mostly alone in the temples and gardens, and to the silence that was only deepened by the loud cawing of crows. So it was a surprise when, having passed through the monumental entrance gate of Nanzen-ji, I ran into a large group of Japanese women chatting happily together in singsong fashion on the covered walkway that led to the abbot's residence. They were all outfitted in elegant silk kimonos, and everything about them, from the ornate inlaid combs in their hair to their gathered obi belts and their pat-terned drawstring purses, was out of another age. The only exception were the dull-brown slippers on their feet, the same kind offered at the entrance of every temple in Kyoto, all of which were tiny and reminded me of the shoes Peter Rabbit lost in the lettuce patch. I'd tried them myself the day before, shoving my feet into them and gripping on with my toes while attempting to slide across the smooth wooden floors, but after almost breaking my neck trying to climb stairs in them, I'd given up and taken to walking across the icy planks in my socks. This made it impossible to ever get warm, and, shivering in my sweater and coat, I wondered how the women didn't freeze wearing only silk, and whether assistance was needed to tie and wrap and secure all the necessary parts of their kimonos.

Without noticing, bit by bit I'd worked my way into the center of the group, so that when suddenly the women began to move in unison, as if in response to some secret signal, I was swept along down the wide and dim open-air corridor, carried by the flow of silk and the hurried pit-patter of tiny slippers. About twenty feet down the walkway, the group came to a halt and spat out from its amoeba-like body a woman dressed in normal street clothes, who now began to address the others. By standing on my tiptoes, I could just see over the women's heads to the four-hundred-year-old Zen garden that was one of the most famous in all of Japan. A Zen garden, with its raked gravel and minimum of rocks, bushes, and trees, is not meant to be entered but to be contemplated from the outside, and just beyond where the group had stopped was the empty portico designed for this. But when I tried to make my way out by tapping shoulders and asking to be excused, the group seemed only to tighten around me. Whomever I tapped would turn to me with a bewildered look, and take a few quick little steps to the left or right so that I could pass, but immediately another woman in a kimono would flood in to fill the void, either out of an innate instinct to right the group's balance or just to get closer to the tour guide. Enclosed on all sides, breathing in the dizzying stench of perfume, and listening to the guide's relentlessly incomprehensible explanations, I began to feel claustrophobic. But before I could try to elbow my way out more violently, the group suddenly began to move again, and by flattening myself against the wall of the abbot's residence I managed to stay put, forcing them to move around me. They crossed the wooden floor in a chorus of scuffling slippers.

It was then that I saw him making his way along the covered walkway in the opposite direction. He looked older, and his wavy hair had turned silver, making his dark eyebrows seem even more severe. Something else was different, too. In the film, it had been absolutely necessary to project the impression of his physical solidity, which Kiarostami had done by keeping the camera closely trained on Ershadi's broad shoulders and strong torso as he drove through the hills outside Tehran. Even when Ershadi got out of the car to gaze out at the arid hills and the camera hung back at a distance, he'd appeared physically formidable, and this had given him a strength and authority that, combined with the depth of feeling in his eyes, had made me want to weep. But now, as he continued down the covered walkway, Ershadi looked almost slender. He'd lost weight, but it was more than that: it seemed that the width of his shoulders had contracted. Now that I was seeing him from the back, I began to doubt that it was Ershadi. But just as disappointment began to pour into me like concrete, the man stopped and turned, as if someone had called to him. He stood very still, looking back at the Zen garden, where the stones were meant to symbolize tigers, leaping toward a place they would never reach. A soft light fell on his expressionless face. And there it was again: the brink of hopelessness. At that moment, I was filled with such overwhelmingly tender feeling that I can only call it love.

Gracefully, Ershadi turned the corner. Unlike me, he had no trouble moving in those slippers. I started to go after him, but one of the kimonoed women appeared to block my path. She was waving and gesturing toward the group, which was now peering into one of the shadowy rooms of the abbot's house. I don't speak Japanese, I explained, trying to get around her, but she kept hopping in front of me, gibbering away and pointing with more and more insistence at the group, which had now begun to move down the hall toward the anterior garden—move with an almost imperceptible shuffle of their combined feet, as if, in fact, thousands of ants were carrying them along. I'm not with the tour, I said, making a little cross with my wrists, which I had seen the Japanese do when they wanted to signal that something was wrong, or not possible, or even forbidden. I was just on my way out, I said, and pointed toward the exit with the same insistence with which the woman in the kimono was pointing at the group.

She grabbed my elbow and was trying to pull me forcibly back in the other direction. Maybe I had upset the delicate balance of the whole, a balance determined by subtleties that I, in my foreignness, would never understand. Or perhaps I had committed an unpardonable act by leaving the group. Again I had the feeling of impenetrable ignorance, which for me will always be synonymous with traveling in Japan. Sorry, I said, but I really have to go now, and with a tug more violent than I'd intended, I freed myself of her hand and jogged toward the exit. But when I turned the corner, there was no sign of Ershadi. The reception area was vacant except for the Japanese women's shoes lined up on the old wooden shelves. I ran outside and looked around, but the temple grounds were occupied only by large crows, which took clumsily to the sky as I ran past.

Love: I can only call it that, however different it was from every other instance of love I had experienced. What I knew of love had always stemmed from desire, from the wish to be altered or thrown off course by an uncontrollable force. But in my love for Ershadi I nearly didn't exist beyond that great feeling. To call it compassion makes it sound like a form of divine love, but it wasn't that, it was terribly human. If anything, it was an animal love, an animal that has been living in an incomprehensible world until one day it encounters another of its kind and understands that it has been applying its comprehension in the wrong place all along.

It sounds far-fetched, but at that moment I had the feeling that I could save Ershadi. Still running, I passed under the monumental wooden gate, and my footfalls echoed up in the rafters. A sense of fear began to seep in, the fear that he planned to take his life just like the character he'd barely played, and that I had lost the brief chance I'd been given to intercede. When I reached the street, it was deserted. I turned in the direction of the famous pathway alongside the narrow river and ran, my bag slapping against my thigh. What would I have said if I had caught up to him? What would I have asked him about devotion? What was it I wanted to be when he turned, and at last his gaze fell upon me? It didn't matter, because when I came around the bend the path was empty, the trees black and bare. Back at the *ryokan*, hunched on the tatami floor, I searched online, but there was no news about Homayoun Ershadi, nothing to suggest that he was traveling in Japan, or no longer alive.

My doubt only grew on the flight back to Tel Aviv. The plane glided above a great shelf of cloud, and the farther it got from Japan, the less possible it seemed that it had actually been Ershadi, until at last it seemed absurd, just as kimonos and Japanese toilets and etiquette and tea ceremonies, which had all possessed irrevocable genius in Kyoto, at a distance grew absurd.

THE NIGHT AFTER I got back to Tel Aviv, I met Romi at a bar. I told her about what had happened in Japan, but in a laughing way: laughing at myself for believing for even a moment that it was actually Ershadi I'd seen and run after. As I told the story, her large eyes became larger. With all of the drama of the actress that she is, Romi lifted a hand to her heart and called the waiter to refill her glass, touching his shoulder in the instinctive way she has of drawing others into her world, under the spell of her intensity. Eyes locked with mine, she removed her cigarettes from her bag, lit one, and inhaled. She reached across the table and laid her hand over my hand. Then she tilted her chin and blew out the smoke, all without breaking her gaze.

I don't believe it, she said at last in a throaty whisper. The exact same thing happened to me.

I began to laugh again. Crazy things were always happening to Romi: her life was swept along by an endless series of coincidences and mystical signs. She was an actress but was not a performer, the difference being that at heart she believed that nothing was real, that everything was a kind of game, but her belief in this was sincere, deep, and true, and her feeling for life was enormous. In other words, she didn't live to convince others of anything. The crazy things that happened to her happened because she opened herself to them and sought them out, because she was always trying something without being too invested in the outcome, only in the feeling it provoked and her ability to rise to it. In her films she was only ever herself, a self stretched this way or that by the circumstances of the script. In the year that we had been friends, I had never known her to lie.

Come on, I said, you're not serious. But as she was never less than completely serious, even while laughing, Romi, still gripping my hand across the table, launched into her own story about Ershadi.

She had seen *Taste of Cherry* five or six years ago in London. Like me, she had been utterly moved by the film and Ershadi's face. Disturbed, even. And yet, at the last moment, she had been released into joy. Yes, joy would be a better word for what she had felt, walking home from the theater in the twilight to her father's apartment. He was dying of cancer, and she had come to take care of him. Her parents had divorced when she was three, and during her childhood and teenage years she and her father had grown distant, and very nearly estranged. But after the army she had gone through a kind of depression and her father had come to see her in the hospital, and the more he sat with her at her bedside, the more she forgave him for the things she had held against him all those years. From then on, they had remained close. She had often gone to stay with him in London, and for a little while even attended acting school there and lived with him in his apartment in Belsize Park. A few years later his cancer had been diagnosed, and a long battle ensued that looked to have been won, until at some point it became clear, beyond a shadow of a doubt, that it had been lost. The doctors gave him three months to live.

Romi left everything in Tel Aviv and moved back to her father's apartment, and during the months that his body began to shut down she stayed by his side, rarely leaving him. He had decided against having any more of the poisonous treatments that would have prolonged his life by only a matter of weeks or months. He wished to die with dignity and in peace, though no one ever really dies in peace, as the body's journey toward the extinction of life always requires violence. These large and small forms of violence were the stuff of their days, but always mingled with her father's humor. They took walks while he could still walk, and when he couldn't anymore they spent long hours watching detective series and nature documentaries. Seeing her father's transfixed expression in the glow of the TV, it struck Romi that he was no less deeply invested in these stories, the stories of unsolved murders, spies, and the uphill battle of a dung beetle trying to roll its ball of manure over a hill, now that his own story was quickly drawing to a close. Too weak to get out of bed to go to the bathroom at night, he would try anyway, and then Romi would hear him collapse on the floor and would go and cradle his head and pick him up, because by then he was no heavier than a child.

It was around this time, the time that her father could no longer make it even the short distance to the bathroom, and the round-the-clock nurse had to throw him over her large Ukrainian shoulder, that, at the nurse's insistence, Romi pulled on her coat and left the house for a few hours to go to see a film. She didn't know anything about it, but she had been drawn to the title, which she had seen on the marquee on a trip to or from the hospital.

She took a seat toward the back of the nearly empty theater. There were only five or six people there, Romi said, but, unlike when the theater is full and everyone disappears around you as the screen comes alive, she felt acutely aware of the presence of the others, most of whom had also come alone. During the many wordless stretches of the film, stretches in which one hears car horns and the sound of bulldozers and the laughter of unseen children, and the long shots when the camera rests on Ershadi's face, Romi felt aware of herself watching, and the others also watching. At the moment she understood that Mr. Badii was planning to take his life and that he was looking for someone to bury him in the morning, she began to cry. Soon after that, a woman stood up and walked out of the theater, and this made Romi feel a little bit better, since it created an unspoken bond between those who had remained.

I wrote that I wouldn't give away the end, but now I see that there is no way around it, that I will have to, since it was Romi's belief that if the film had come to a normal end, what happened to each of us later almost certainly would not have happened. That is, if, after presumably swallowing the pills and putting on a light jacket against the cold, Mr. Badii had just lain down in the ditch that he'd dug, and everything had grown dim as we watched his impassive face watching the full moon sail in and out from behind the smoky clouds, and then, as a clap of thunder sounded, when it had grown so dark that we could no longer see him at all until a flash of lightning illuminated the screen again and there he was, still lying there, staring out, still of this world, still waiting, as we are still waiting, only to be plunged into darkness again until the next bright flash in which we'd discover that his eyes have at last drifted closed, and then the screen turned black for good, leaving only the sound of rain falling harder and harder, until finally it crescendoed and faded away—if the film had just ended there, as it seemed to have every intention of doing, then, Romi said, it might not have stayed with her.

But the film did not end there. Instead, the rhythmic chanting of marching soldiers drifts in, and slowly the screen comes to life again. This time, when the hilly landscape comes into view, it's spring, everything is green, and the grainy, discolored footage is shot on video. The soldiers march in formation onto the winding road in the lower left corner of the screen. This new view is surprising enough, but a moment later a member of the film's crew appears, carrying the camera toward another man, who is setting up a tripod, and then Ershadi himself—Ershadi, whom we just saw fall asleep in his grave—casually walks into the frame, wearing light, summery clothes. He takes a cigarette from his front pocket, lights it between his lips, and without a word hands it to Kiarostami, who accepts it without pausing his conversation with the DP, and without so much as looking at Ershadi, who in that moment we understand is connected to him through a channel of pure intuition. The shot cuts to the soundman, a little farther down the hill, crouching down out of the wind in the high grass with his giant microphone.

Can you hear me? a disembodied voice asks.

Down below the drill sergeant falters and ceases his shouting. *Bâlé?* he says. Yes?

Tell your men to stay near the tree to rest, Kiarostami replies. The shoot is over. The last line of the film is spoken a few moments later as Louis Armstrong's mournful trumpet starts to wail, and the soldiers can be seen sitting and laughing and talking and gathering flowers by the tree where Mr. Badii lay down in the hope of eternal rest, though now the tree is covered with green leaves.

We're here for the sound take, Kiarostami says.

And then it is just that huge, beautiful, plaintive trumpet, without words. Romi sat through the trumpet and credits, and, though tears were streaming down her face, she felt elated.

It was not until some time after she had laid her father in the ground, and shoveled the dirt into his grave herself, pushing away her uncle, who tried to pry the tool from her, that Romi recalled Ershadi. So many intense things had happened to her since she walked home full of joy in the twilight that she hadn't had time to think about the film again. She had stayed on in London to take care of her father's things, and when there was nothing left to take care of, when everything had been finalized and squared away, she remained in the nearly empty apartment for months.

During the days, all of which passed in the same way, she lay around listlessly, unable to apply herself to anything. The only place she could feel any desire was during sex, and so she had started seeing Mark again, a man she had dated during the year she was at acting school. He was possessive, which is part of why their relationship had ended in the first place. And now that she had been with other men since they'd broken up, he was even more jealous and obsessive, and wouldn't stop pushing her to tell him what it had been like with them. But the sex they had was hard and good, and she found it bracing after the months of feeling like she had no body, when her father's failing body was the only body there was.

At night, after Mark came home from work, Romi would go to his place, and in the darkened bedroom he would scroll through pornography until he found what he was looking for, and then would fuck her from behind as she lay on her stomach and they watched two or three men penetrating one woman on the massive screen of his TV, pushing their dicks into her pussy and her ass and her mouth, everyone breathing and moaning in surround sound. Just before he came, Mark would slap Romi hard on the ass, thrusting himself into her and calling her a whore, enacting some ancient pain that drove him to believe that the woman he loved would never remain true to him. One night after this performance Mark had fallen asleep with his arms around her, and Romi had lain awake, for, exhausted as she always was, she couldn't sleep. Finally she shimmied out from under him and crawled around on the floor in search of her underwear. Having no desire to stay, and no desire to go, she'd sunk back down on the edge of Mark's bed and felt the remote under her. She switched on the TV and surfed the channels, passed over the stories of mother elephants and bee colonies that she had watched with her father, over the cold cases and the late-night talk shows, until she pushed the button once more and there, nearly filling the enormous screen, was Ershadi's face. For a second it appeared larger than life in the otherwise dark room, and then it was lost again, because her thumb had continued its restless search before she realized what she was seeing. When she flipped back, she couldn't find him. There was nothing on about film, or Iran, or Kiarostami. She sat there, startled and bewildered in the dark, and then slowly a sense of longing came over her like a wave, and she started to laugh for the first time since her father had died, and she knew it was time to go home.

THERE WAS NO choice but to believe Romi. Her story was so precise that she couldn't have made it up. Sometimes she exaggerated the details, but she did it believing the exaggerations, and this only made her more lovable, because it showed you what she could do with the raw material of the world. And yet, after I went home and the spell of her presence wore off, I lay on my bed feeling sad and empty and increasingly depressed, since not only was my encounter with Ershadi not unique, but, worse, unlike Romi, I'd had no idea what it meant, or what I was supposed to do with it. I had failed to understand anything, or take anything from it, and had told the story as a joke, laughing at myself. Lying alone in the dark, I started to cry. Sick of the pain throbbing in my ankle, I swallowed a handful of Advil in the bathroom. The pills swilled in my stomach with the wine I'd drunk, and soon enough nausea overtook me, and then I was kneeling on the bathroom floor, throwing up into the toilet.

The next morning, I woke to banging on the door. Romi had had a sense that something was wrong and had tried to call, but I hadn't picked up all night. Still woozy, I started to cry again. Seeing the state I was in, she went into high gear, boiling tea, laying me out on the couch, and cleaning up my face. She held my hand, her other palm resting on her own throat, as if my pain were her pain, and she felt everything and understood everything.

Two months later I quit the company. I enrolled in graduate school at NYU, but stayed on in Tel Aviv through the summer, and flew back only days before the start of the semester. Romi had met Amir by then, an entrepreneur fifteen years older than her, with so much money that he spent most of his time looking for ways to give it away. He wooed Romi with the same singular drive he applied to everything he wanted. A few days before my flight, Romi threw a goodbye party for me at our favorite restaurant, and all the dancers came, and our friends, and most of the boys we'd slept with that year. Amir didn't come because he was busy, and the following day Romi left for Sardinia on his yacht. I packed up my things alone. I was sad to leave and wondered if I'd made a mistake.

For a while, we stayed in close touch. Romi got married, moved to Amir's mansion on a cliff above the Mediterranean, and got pregnant. I studied toward my degree and fell in love, and then out of it a couple of years later. In the meantime, Romi had two children, and sometimes she sent me photos of those boys, whose faces were hers and seemed to borrow nothing from their father. But we were in touch less and less, and then whole years passed in which we didn't speak at all. One day, soon after my daughter was born, I was passing a cinema on Twelfth Street and I felt someone's gaze, and when I turned I saw Ershadi's eyes staring out at me from the poster for *Taste of Cherry*. I felt a shiver up my spine. The screening had already passed, but no one had taken down the poster. I took a photo of it, and that night I sent it to Romi, reminding her of a plan we'd once hatched to go to Tehran—me with a fresh American passport without Israeli stamps, and her with the British one she had through her father—to sit in the cafés and walk the streets that were the setting of so many films we loved, to taste life there, and lie on the beaches of the Caspian Sea. We were going to find Ershadi, who we imagined would invite us into the sleek apartment he had designed himself and listen while we told him our stories, and then tell us his own while we drank black tea with a view of the snow-capped Elburz Mountains. In the letter, I admitted to her the reason I'd cried the night she told me about her encounter with Ershadi. Sooner or later, I wrote, I would've had to admit that in the blaze of my ambition, I'd failed to check myself. I would have had to face how miserable I was, and how confused my feelings about dancing had become. But the desire to seize something from Ershadi, to feel that reality expanded for me as it had for her, that the other world came through to touch me, had hastened my revelations.

I DIDN'T HEAR back from Romi for weeks, and then finally her answer arrived. She apologized for taking so long. It was strange, she said. She hadn't thought of Ershadi for years, until three months before, when she'd decided to watch *Taste of Cherry* again. She'd recently left Amir, and on nights when she couldn't sleep in the new apartment, with its unfamiliar smells and noises from the street, she would stay up watching movies. What surprised her was how differently Ershadi's character struck her this time. While she'd remembered him as passive, nearly saintlike, now she saw that he was impatient and often surly with the men he approached, and manipulative in the way he tried to get them to agree to what he wanted, sizing up their vulnerabilities and saying whatever was necessary to convince them. His focus on his own misery, and his single-minded desire to carry out his plan, struck her as self-absorbed. What also surprised her, because she didn't remember it, were the words that appear for a moment on the black screen before the film begins, as all films in Iran must: "In the name of God." How could she have missed that the first time? she wondered. Of course she'd thought of me as she lay in the dark and watched—of that year when we were still so young and spoke endlessly of men. How much time we wasted, she wrote, believing that things came to us as gifts, through channels of wonder, in the form of signs, in the love of men, in the name of God, rather than seeing them for what they were: strengths we dragged up from the nothingness of our own depths. She told me about a film she wanted to write when she finally got the time, which followed the story of a dancer like me. And then she told me about her boys, who needed her for everything, it seemed, just as the men in her life had always needed her for everything. It was good, she wrote, that I had a daughter. And then, as if she had forgotten that she had already moved on to other things, as if we were still sitting across from each other deep in one of our conversations without beginning, middle, or end, Romi wrote that the last thing that had surprised her was that when Ershadi is lying in the grave he's dug and his eyes finally drift closed and the screen goes black, it isn't really black at all. If you look closely, you can see the rain falling.

Future Emergencies

For a long time they said we didn't need them, but then something changed and they said that we did: gas masks. This was after 9/11, after the establishment of Homeland Security, when the factory of America's imagination had achieved its peak production of threats, attacks, conspiracies. I was standing barefoot in the kitchen, listening to the radio turned up loudly, as I liked to do in the morning. The radio! It gives the news a greater impact, and increases the drama of beginning another day in a world I've grown used to but know can change at any moment. When the announcement was made, my first instinct was to hold my breath in case whatever it was had already been released into the air. "What?" Victor asked, coming in and turning down the volume. I exhaled. "Gas masks," I said.

But outside the window, the morning was pale and clear. There appeared to be nothing in the atmosphere beyond the invisible blessing of oxygen. Other things too, equally invisible: a trace of benzene, a low-level reading of mercury or dioxin maybe. But nothing we hadn't learned to live with. Sometimes at dusk I watch runners on the track around the reservoir, their lungs pumping to take in the maximum cubic feet of air, and the thought occurs to me that maybe they belong to a more evolved subspecies, one actually benefiting from—actually able to break down and harness for energy—elements still toxic to the rest of us. Victor calls it the flagellation parade. He says that they're wearing away their joints, grinding down cartilage. He says they'll leave the world limping or crawling on all fours. But to me they seem the image of health: lithe, agile, unharmed by pollution. They know it makes the sunsets more beautiful, all of those particles in the air. The sky turns colors that seem to reflect the peculiar ache of being alive at that hour.

"The threat may not come from common pollutants or shifting winds," the radio said. "It may not come from airborne pesticides, or a factory fire, or underground tests." The coffee-maker purred, and Victor took two mugs off the shelf. "Where will the threat come from?" I asked aloud. I felt an intimate connection to the voice, at liberty to ask it questions. "The threat may come from an unknown source," the radio replied. Even when the news is bad, I am glad to have been answered.

For the time being, the air was still safe to breathe, the radio said. It was all right to go outside, remembering to stop and get a mask at one of the distribution centers being set up in each neighborhood. Victor had been planning on staying in to grade papers, so I offered to pick up masks for both of us on my way back from work.

"If there's a choice, I'd like the kind with the eyeholes and the snout. The anteater one," Victor said, going to the door for the newspaper.

"I don't think this is a time to be picky."

"True," said Victor, already absorbed in reading.

It was November, and outside the air was crisp and seemed to carry the promise of snow. What I miss about living in the country is the morbid beauty of the autumns. In the city the leaves just turn brown and scatter. Once I took Victor back to the farm where I grew up, and it rained the whole time. We tramped around in the mud and I tried to show him how to milk a cow, but he couldn't stand the smell of the hot milk. When we finally left, he said that one had to have a sense of humor to grow up in a place like that. I didn't explain to him how the dogs used to come into the house smelling of the fields.

I met Victor in my last year of college. He was the professor of my medieval history class. Victor is French, and so he didn't have any hang-ups about going out with a student. After graduation I moved in with him and got a job giving tours at the Metropolitan Museum. Though the life we live together now feels like the only one I know, there are moments when I still imagine another life, with different things in it. A life with someone who is not Victor, and who is nothing like him.

On the steps down to the subway I passed a man coming up wearing a gas mask. It wasn't the kind Victor was talking about. This one was fancier, with circles over the nose and mouth and on each cheek, the one on the left twice the size of the others, like a goiter. The man was wearing a red silk tie and a suit that looked like it had just been unwrapped from the dry cleaner.

The sight of him was unnerving, and people stopped to stare. Some probably hadn't heard the news that morning, and the ones that had were wondering if there had been an update. There had been warnings before about the possible need for the masks, but this was the first time they were actually being distributed, and obviously it set everyone on edge. When I went down to the subway platform, there were a few people who'd already gone to the distribution centers and were carrying their masks in cardboard boxes. I thought about going to pick ours up, but I was late for work and the first tour of the day is always my favorite. The light comes in softly through the skylights, illuminating the Madonnas and the saints.

There were only five people in my morning tour: a couple from Texas, a mother and daughter from Munich, and a cellist named Paul. He had beautiful hands. I noticed them when he touched his forehead. Everyone was feeling a little nervous, and we spent the first few minutes talking about the news in the hushed tones used in museums. When the group is small, I usually ask the visitors what they're interested in and try to tailor the tour to their tastes. The man from Texas had a gold ring on his pinkie and said he was a big fan of Renoir. He pronounced it *Rin-Waa*, and his wife smiled in agreement.

Paul was interested in the museum's photography collection, so I started off in the room with the Walker Evanses. I've always been struck by his photographs, their sparse and formal beauty. Here were these people caught in grim and hopeless lives, and he photographed them with the same precise detachment he would an old signboard. There's something breathtaking about it, the lack of compassion in favor of cold clarity. There were a couple of photographs by Diane Arbus at the other end of the room, and I decided to show them to the group to give them a sense of the other end of the spectrum, someone who seemed to identify with her subjects on a terrifying level. Not only does Arbus seem to feel their unhappiness, I explained, but what's more, they—the twins and the triplets, the misfit children, the odd couples, the tramps, the queens and freaks—seem to regard *her* with distraught looks, as if they recognize something darker and more haunting than their own lot. Sometimes, on a good day, that happens: as you talk, you find things you didn't know you had to say.

I let the group look for a while in silence at the child clutching the toy grenade and the old woman in a wheelchair holding a witch's mask over her face. I was a little worried about how the man from Texas would react, but I should have given him the benefit of the doubt because he ended up taking a big interest, going right up close and screwing up his face in concentration. Paul had drifted back over to the Walker Evanses. His hands made me think of delicate, impossible tasks. They made me think, I don't know why, of a man on the flight that crashed into the icy Potomac, in whose pocket was found a picture of the woman he loved and a pair of laminated butterfly wings.

Before Victor I always dated men my own age. It's hard to remember what they were like now, the smoothness of their skin, and how when I took my clothes off they seemed almost grateful. It's even hard to remember what it felt like to be the person they loved, for whom the world was still opening. A person who is not, in some form, a refraction of Victor. When I first met him, I was practically a kid. He struck me as strong and utterly remarkable, a man against whose finished form I could lean to feel the pleasure of a permanent shape.

While I was eating lunch, one of the other guides, Ellen, who was thin and had a long neck, came into the staff room. She'd already picked up her mask, and put it on as a joke. She got right up in my face like the Texan in front of the Arbus, and peered down at me through the eyeholes. I let out a playful scream, but the truth was that the way she looked, like a giant praying mantis, gave me the creeps. Ellen started to bark with laughter, the sound trapped and muffled by the rubber mouthpiece. Then she pushed the mask back onto her head and finished the rest of her tuna-fish sandwich with the eyeholes staring blindly up at the ceiling. Sometimes Ellen and I talk about our relationships. Her boyfriend rock-climbs, calls her Lou, and got arrested for scalping tickets to *Riverdance*. She says I'm lucky to have a man with such refined taste, who has dedicated his life to the pursuit of ideas.

Victor's sense of humor is also unusual. He's a medievalist, which already suggests something about his tastes, but add to that the fact that he wrote his dissertation on the penal system in thirteenth-century Burgundy, and you begin to have a real sense of what a person like Victor might find funny. When we first started dating, I found the blackness of his humor charming. It drew attention to the difference in our ages, leaving me free to take on the role of the naive, uncorrupted youth. Soon Victor will be forty-five. When he doesn't shave, some of the hairs in his beard come in silver, and sometimes, lying with my cheek against his, a sense of gratitude still comes over me and I love him more than ever. I have the feeling then that Victor is standing between me and some distant harm, and that his presence is what shields me from it. I curl myself up in his arms like a cat, and when he asks why I'm being so affectionate I only smile and rub my eyelid against the pleasant roughness of his chin.

My last tour at the museum ended at a quarter to five, and I got my coat and headed outside. The clocks had been turned back a week earlier, and I still hadn't gotten used to the dark coming in so early. I always feel a little pang of hurt that first day when darkness falls without warning. It's the slight, sickening feeling of being reminded of the reckless authority of time, of losing your bearings in a world whose dimensions you thought you'd learned to live with. I took my time getting back. I imagined Paul practicing somewhere in an empty auditorium. The park was emptier than usual, but the runners were still out, sprinting under the bare trees around the reservoir, the light from the lamps shining off the reflector guards on their sneakers and clothing.

The distribution center for our neighborhood was an elementary school on a quiet street of town houses. There were paper cutouts of turkeys and pilgrims in the window. When I got there, people were bustling in and out, gathering in little clots on the steps to share whatever they knew. Judging from what I overheard on the way in, it wasn't much. At work I'd heard various speculations—the man from Texas thought that there had been some sort of meltdown at a nuclear plant, and Ellen insisted that a crop duster from Colombia had disappeared—but none were particularly credible. It seemed strange that no one was explaining the sudden need for gas masks, and also that the city had been prepared with enough masks on hand for every-one. But I assumed there were reasons. Victor says that I don't question things enough. He says I accept the way things are without challenge. The first words he ever directed at me were written on the top of an essay I'd handed in. "Your argument is unclear," he wrote. "See me."

The distribution was set up in one of the classrooms. There was a master list with all of the residents' names, and when I got to the front of the line for J through P, I had to explain that I was also picking one up for Victor Assoulen, and could I please have his without having to stand in the line for A through F. There was a small bureaucratic scuffle among the volunteers working on the other side of the blockade of children's desks, but after I showed them an ID with an address that matched Victor's, it got straightened out, and a woman in a velour track-suit handed me two boxes. On my way out I stopped to smile at a little girl hopping around in ballet slippers, and when I looked up again I noticed a note left on the blackboard. It read, in elegant teacher's cursive, "Due Monday: Your predictions for the future." I started to laugh, but caught myself when I turned back and met the cool gaze of the small prophet in scuffed bal-let slippers.

Ask Victor, and he'll tell you that the Middle Ages were more passionate times than these. Extreme contrasts and violent con-flicts existed side by side, lending a thrilling vigor to life that order can't provide. He'll sit with you over a bottle of wine and explain to you in a breathlessly articulate manner how now all anyone wants is conflict resolution. They want to shake hands and settle matters; they want tolerance for all points of view, so long as those points of view are expressed through the proper channels and procedures. It's not that Victor would have us all back in the thirteenth century, cheering in spasmodic effusion at public executions. His sense of morality is finely tuned. But he refuses to accept a system designed to reject conflict and force us all, like a fat lady through a keyhole, in the direction of a stable average. That's the phrase he uses, a fat lady through a keyhole.

When I got home, Victor was standing in the kitchen knee-deep in shopping bags. He'd bought more food than we normally eat in a month, and was trying to find room for it all in our tiny kitchen. When he saw me standing in the door, he put down a jar of peanut butter he was trying to wedge between some soup cans, waded across the sea of plastic bags, and hugged me hard. Normally when I come home Victor peeks out from behind some book about minstrels and barely raises an eyebrow. It's not that he isn't glad to see me; he just likes to greet me in his own time. It's as if there are two Victors, and between the intellectual Victor engaged in an ongoing critique of the suppression of conflict and the Victor who rubs my toes when I'm cold there is a powerful force field, and each day, like a superhero morphing back into his normal life, Victor must cross back through it to get me.

"Hi," I said into the flannel of his shirt.

"I was worried," said Victor. "I tried to call you at the museum to come home early."

"Why? Was there more news? Why didn't you call my cell phone?"

I'd had the phone since a month after 9/11; my father had

insisted. But he and my mother were the only ones who called me on it. Victor did not yet believe in being reached.

"No. They're giving instructions on how to seal the windows with duct tape, but they're not saying why. I went to the supermarket."

We both looked around the kitchen at the bags of apricots and pears, the cheese wrapped in butcher paper, the loaves of bread, the chocolate bars and pints of ice cream, the cold cuts and condiments, the plastic tubs of dips and spreads.

"I can see."

"The store was being emptied. I grabbed what I could," Victor said. "I'm going to make you dinner," he said, nipping my ear between his lips.

Victor is a talented cook, and in the ten minutes it took me to change into my sweatpants and curl up on the sofa in front of the TV, the apartment was already filled with the smell of something good simmering on the stove. I watched as the news channel flashed images of ransacked shelves at the supermarkets and lines snaking out onto the street outside the distribution centers, and then the picture cut to a little girl with blond curls and a nose crusted with snot trying to work a gas mask down over her face. When I looked up from the TV screen I caught a reflection of myself in the window, tucked under a blanket like a child before a hurricane, and I realized that I was full of happy anticipation. Outside the world was cold and dark, but inside the rooms were lit with the yellow glow of lamps, and, waiting for Victor to call me for dinner, I felt the rush of pleasure that I used to seek in the made-up games of my childhood, where all things were eclipsed by the singular goal of survival.

Victor must have felt it too, because despite the grim uncertainty of the news and the future threat of scarcity, the meal he'd prepared was a feast. We ate Japanese style, sitting on cushions around the coffee table, the television turned down low behind us. There was duck cooked with apricots and raspberries, and salad with pomegranate seeds. He turned off the lights, lit candles, and opened a bottle of wine from the region where his family comes from in Languedoc. I told him about the scene at the distribution center. He stopped eating and stared at me the way he used to when I was a student and would sit in his office scratching my bare knees. In the middle of a sentence he leaned across the corner of the table and kissed me. His tongue was in my mouth, and he slipped his hand under my bra. When I pushed my hand against the hardness under his jeans, he groaned and rolled on top of me. He unbuckled his belt, and I inhaled sharply when he pulled off my pants and I felt him against my stomach, felt my spine crack, and my ribs pressing into the floorboards.

We ate dessert flushed and damp with sweat. It had been a long time since we'd done something like that. Despite Victor's interest in the passion of the Middle Ages, his campaign in favor of friction and conflict, even he would have to admit that our own relationship was closer to the stable average of which he was so critical. We'd been living together for five years, and our days and nights had taken on a certain familiar order dictated by my hours at the museum and Victor's at the university, and the great, silent country of hours that Victor spent at work in his study.

The candles were burning deep, their centers already liquid.

Victor shared out what was left of the wine into our glasses, and even though I was already feeling a little drunk, I swallowed mine down in a couple of gulps. We turned up the news again and listened, but there wasn't any new information, just the same images, over and over, of people trying on gas masks and walking around with them as if they were testing the feel of new shoes. Neither of us was tired, or maybe we didn't want the evening to end, didn't want to go to sleep and wake up to whatever the world would bring us tomorrow, so we decided to play a game of Scrabble. Victor is obsessed with the game and must know every three-letter word in the language. It helps that his English is impeccable. My ear is so used to his accent that there are times when I almost forget that most of Victor's life took place in another idiom, with different expressions for pleasure and pain, in sentences to me foreign and incomprehensible. Sometimes I come across Victor exclaiming aloud to himself in French, and I am reminded of this other life, for a moment thrown off guard, and forced to add a third, secret Victor to the Victors I already know.

While Victor went to get the Scrabble board I cleared our plates, piling them in the sink with the dirty pots and pans in which the remains of our dinner were already congealing. The sight of them gave me a vague nauseated feeling. On the way back to the living room I passed the boxes with our gas masks where I'd left them sitting by the door. I picked them up and carried them over to the sofa, one under each arm, and while Victor was setting up the board I opened them. I pulled one out of the wrapping, and the instructions fluttered to the floor.

"Look," I said, holding it up. It was the kind Victor had asked

for, the basic kind everyone was getting with large round eyeholes and a short trunk over the mouth.

"Let me see." Victor turned it over in his hands and examined it. He pulled the bands back and slipped it over his face,
then turned and regarded me calmly through the clear plastic lenses. He looked ugly and menacing, a strange creature I'd
never seen before who was Victor nonetheless, and I felt a flash
of anger rise to my cheeks. Without thinking, I leaned forward
and blasted each eyehole with a shot of breath, fogging his view.
For a moment neither of us moved. Victor continued to sit in
silence, and I watched as the clouds of breath slowly evaporated,
revealing his distant, dull pupils. Then, at last, when his view
had cleared entirely, he winked.

"Take it off," I demanded. Victor was motionless, as if the
mask had made him demented. "*Take it off.*" My heart was beat-
ing fast. I felt a fierce urge to kick him, but I was sitting down.
Before I could do anything, he slipped it off his face and laid it
on the floor.

"It stinks of rubber," he said. Then he went about choosing
his seven letters. I watched his face in silence, surprised at myself.

Victor put down *lemur* for the first word, to which I added
nut, and then Victor did *geek* and I did *guns*. Everything was
fine for a while, the little crux of wooden letters expanding like
some kind of self-multiplying message, garbled at first but, if
you looked carefully enough using the right decoder, possessing
its own intelligence, its subtle eloquence, *neck* sprouting from
geek and *lick* from *neck* like some kind of confused desire trapped
in the language with nothing to do but try desperately to spell

its want. Maybe it was just the wine, but as we played I started to think that if we tried hard enough, we could figure out what it was that we were trying to say to each other after all these years, after all the pages read and the meals eaten and the silences kept, and then he put down *positron*, and all of a sudden I realized that I wanted to tell Victor that I was thinking of leaving him.

Victor won, as he often does, and as he was dumping the letters back into the drawstring pouch, I began to cry. At first Victor didn't notice, but at last he glanced up, and a look of surprise crossed his face.

"It's only a game," he joked.

I tried to smile and shook my head. I wanted to tell him about what I'd realized about the Arbus photographs, about the old woman in a wheelchair who lifted a witch's mask to her face when the shutter clicked, maybe to protect herself from the photographer's acute gaze, or send back to Arbus an image of herself, or to throw a wrench into the eternal chain of reflections between two people who gaze upon each other and see, in the stranger looking back, a startling image of themselves. But I said nothing. Victor kneeled in front of me and wiped a tear from my cheek.

"It's okay."

"I'm scared," I whispered.

"It happens," Victor said, taking me in his arms, and yet unwilling, even for a moment, to be anything but pragmatic. "A necessary scourge, natural or man-made, that comes through periodically to control the population."

I looked up at him. I knew he thought that I was frightened of whatever it was that we were waiting to hear news of, the thing that might threaten the very air we breathed and the life we'd grown used to. And maybe I was. Or maybe I was just tired and drunk, fed up with the argument in my head—for or against a life with Victor—that all this time later was still unclear. It was already midnight. The glasses smeared with fingerprints were still on the table, holding the last drops of wine from the place Victor might have come from had his father not moved to Paris to become a doctor, beginning the chain of events that would lead to Victor's childhood spent in the shadow of L'Hôpital Saint-Vincent-de-Paul, his youthful interest in plagues and infectious diseases, his passion for the Middle Ages, his teaching job in America, and, finally, me. One of the candles sputtered and went out, and Victor leaned away from me and blew out the other. He lay on the rug and pulled me down next to him, and we held each other in the blue glow of the television.

And then we fell asleep, sprawled there among the Scrabble letters and the empty wineglasses, and when I woke up again, the sky outside was already starting to lighten. My right hand had fallen asleep, and when I touched it with the fingers of the left the sensation was chilling, like touching the hand of a dead person. I untangled myself from Victor and shook it until the feeling came back. I had a headache, and my mouth was dry, so I got up to get some water from the kitchen. When I came back, the television was mutely flickering, and in its light I saw the gas mask lying on its side by Victor's face. I picked it up and turned it over, and then I slipped it over my face. It was snug inside, safe like a catcher's mask, and I lay down on my back, blinking up through the eyeholes. I wondered how long it would be until we knew what it was we were going to need to learn to protect ourselves from, or if it was too late, if the only ones who would survive were those who had been training all the while, with reflective clothing and superior lungs. Maybe whatever it was had already seeped through the cracks of the windows and the door. But I was drowsy, and too tired to object. Without turning to look, I moved my hand until my fingertips touched Victor's cheek. Then I closed my eyes to wait, grateful for what was left of the dark.

The next morning was Saturday, and we woke up to the news that the whole thing had been some sort of test. Victor perched on the edge of the couch, his hair sticking up as if he had fought a windstorm to make it through to daybreak. He held the coffee mug between his hands and took little sips, his gaze fixed on the television. After I got out of the shower, I sat down next to him. The mayor was giving a press conference, explaining how they'd wanted to make certain that the city was prepared. We were instructed to keep the masks in a safe and dry place where we would be able to find them easily. He apologized for any inconvenience or unnecessary fright the test had caused anyone, thanked all of the volunteers, and congratulated the city for the admirable way it had performed in test conditions. When the reporters began to bark out questions, I went to the kitchen to pour myself some coffee, and when I switched on the radio, the mayor's answers echoed through the apartment in an eerie duet.

It had snowed during the night, which was unusual for that time of year, and Victor and I decided to take a walk together. It had been a long time since we did that, almost as long as since we'd last interrupted dinner to fuck on the living-room floor. It was cold, so we bundled up in hats and scarves, and Victor wore the red wool mittens I'd knitted for him when that was something I did. I wore a pair of gloves that were frayed at the thumbs, and when we stopped to wait for the light to change, Victor lifted my thumb to his mouth like a horn and blew hot air through the hole.

In the park the snow crunched under our feet. The sun had come out and reflected brightly off everything. Victor made a snowball and threw it at a tree, an explosion of whiteness against the black. I kept slipping because my shoes didn't have any treads, but Victor held my arm so I wouldn't fall. There were some kids running around with a dog in the snow, and Victor laughed loudly as he watched.

I thought about that day some weeks later when I did one of those home tests and found out that I was pregnant. I did it twice because the first time the pink line showed up in the box I couldn't believe it, even though I'm never late. For a few days I didn't tell Victor. I went to work and did the tours with the knowledge that in me something tiny was becoming, a kind of human insistence, steadily growing until the day it would finally make its way out into the world to tell us what all this time we had not known, been without, were left wondering. A small being with a clear argument, able to predict the future. Perhaps there was a time during those silent days while I carried around that secret, a small window of opportunity. But it never occurred to me not to keep the baby. During the long months of my pregnancy, before I became too big to walk as far as the park, I often stood outside the fence and watched the runners on the track. I possessed the small, inexplicable hope that if I watched them long enough, the child might be born into their race, with invincible lungs and immunity to whatever it was in the air that drove us to drunkenness and lit the sky at sunset.

Once, on the way there, I passed someone—it was impossible to tell if it was a man or woman—with a gas mask on. Maybe it was a joke, or maybe the person didn't trust the mayor, or maybe he or she had simply gotten used to wearing it, had grown to like it in fact, and was reluctant to part with it now and go back to walking around with a naked face, exposed to everything.

Amour

I knew her when we were young, and then we lost touch for decades until I saw her again in one of the refugee camps. There are faces that suffering changes beyond all recognition. But there are those who possess something, a defining feature maybe, that can't be altered or deformed, not by time, or displacement, or any variety of pain. Sophie's eyes were a deep gray that at times, in certain weather, turned almost violet. When I first saw her thin figure in the line that snaked along the chain-link fence, a blue blanket draped over her shoulders, I couldn't recall her name or even to which of the disjointed epochs of my life she belonged, but I recognized those eyes. Then I heard her voice and I remembered, and for the little while that our paths remained crossed, what I couldn't remember or never knew, she told me.

Back then Sophie hadn't been alone, and despite all the intervening years, with their myriad collapses and disintegrations, I still half expected to see Ezra fly out from the jumble of alleys, bundled in some wretched coat hanging below his knees, wild-bearded, rabbinical and rabid, clutching some loaf or can he'd bartered, or talked his way into, or otherwise Ezra-like negotiated. I'd always liked Sophie, and envied him for having her. And I envied how inevitable their coupling seemed, what a solid fit they made while the rest of us kept coming together and apart, hooking up, falling in love, and then discovering we were only half-baked.

They'd met in New York toward the very end of the 1990s, but well enough before the actual end that by the time it was nigh, they had plans in place to spend it together, to spend New Year's snow camping while all the world's computers glitched, erasing time, rolling us all back to the Stone Age. These two—ever ready for anything, up for anything—would be ready even for this, spooning in their icy white cave or lying just outside it on their backs, in the cupped wings of their own angels, looking up not at the hyperbrilliance of Grucci fireworks but of native stars: stars scattered wild across the universe over Colorado, I think it was, or maybe Wyoming. That neither of them—one raised on the North Shore of Long Island, and the other on an island in South Jersey, both in Congregations Beth Shalom, both in homes kosher but not shomer Shabbat, where being American was an accident of history, English an accident of history, nature an accident of history—that neither of these two had even the faintest notion of how to make a fire, pitch a tent, or waterproof their stuff, let alone survive in subzero temperatures, fazed them not at all, because thus far they had been fantastically, almost mystically competent, not only in getting into good colleges and making their way in the world but also finding beauty in it. That they broke up for the first time before the end of that long, punishing-to-most-but-not-to-them millennium ever arrived was the reason they didn't ultimately snow-camp, it should be said: Not because they couldn't have figured it out. Not because her family, who still made vain gestures of influence, said crazy, said hypothermia. Not because the plane tickets were prohibitively expensive, not to mention all that waterproof gear. Not because either of them stopped believing, even for a second, in the true and the consoling brilliance of those stars.

They broke up over I don't know what, and the pain was terrible, unbearable, at least for Sophie. Though for Ezra, too, I have to think, to lose a woman like her. They didn't have cell phones yet, and the Internet was still dial-up and mostly vacant, and so for a while there was only silence between them, only crying and wondering, not knowing nor being able to know, which is to say: enduring, waiting. The event horizon came and went with each dry, not-freezing, and alone, though at midnight, drunk and feeling ruthless, she turned to the guy who'd been talking her into the wall—me—and kissed him.

But in late February of that fresh year with all the zeroes, they ran into each other in the line outside Film Forum, and apologies were whispered, and more tears were shed, and her hand slid under his jacket and his flannel shirt to touch his bare, warm skin, and soon enough they were back together again, inhaling each other in the old way, because was there anybody else who could love as big as she could, who was as spirited and as honest, and was there anyone as wickedly funny as he was, as avid, as verbose? Was there anyone else who would go see all those Pasolinis and Fellinis with him, or anyone else who would read to her from Martin Buber's *Tales of the Hasidim* over the phone, the cordless one cradled hot against her ear, on those nights when he was downtown and she was uptown and couldn't sleep? That yes, factually, in New York City at the very start of the millennium there were still people who would have done these things, who were doing these things, was irrelevant to their love, just as it was irrelevant, lying anew in each other's arms, that they'd met one spring afternoon in 1999 purely by chance, and that had they not, each would have eventually fallen for another, which meant that each was replaceable, that each could be replaced. From then on they were solidly together—their coupledom was fixed, became a fixture that the rest of us drank at, envied, aspired to.

SO MUCH THE SAME, but with the emphasis in a different place: that was the simple, clockwork beauty of their union, as they saw it. Once, early on, lying naked on the mattress in his East Village apartment, she assessed aloud their compatibility, and he listened and agreed and then put it this way: While she looked for all to see like a nice, good girl who did everything right, in truth she liked transgression and had a dirty mouth and her dark side liked it darker, while *he* presented as dark, troubled, and filthy, but actually was warm and pretty nice. Beyond that, they'd come down from more or less the same number of Holocaust survivors, had more or less the same number of relatives in Israel, each had a mother born in Europe and a father just barely born in America who'd been Republican up to Reagan; each had been raised with the same death-penalty prohibition against marrying a goy, or failing in any way, which is to say that each was a product of the same proud, closed-minded, hotheaded, anxious, comforting, all-consuming tribalism, but while Sophie's mother, resenting the confines of her postwar North London Orthodox childhood, had sent her daughter to public school in Roslyn, he, Ezra, had been sent to, and eventually kicked out of, yeshiva.

Beyond even that, both wanted to be what their families, who had seen so much, had not yet seen: a person who considers it their vocation to make not a living, not money, not measurable success—but art.

Pasolini! I repeated, when Sophie told me this detail. She was lying on her pallet under the dirty, tattered blue blanket, watching the rain dribble into a rusted, overflowing metal drum. I'd forgotten that name, and by then I'd forgotten the images of most of the movies I'd once seen. But Sophie could remember them all. She could describe whole scenes, the light, the camera angles, she could even remember the lines, and when she unspooled these films, her gray-violet eyes softened, as if she were watching them again, projected on the tarpaulin of makeshift tents, the rubbled walls, the filthy sky crosshatched with wires. Whoever was nearby, or waiting with us on the line for the food kits, vaccines, or juice boxes that might or might not come, would quiet down and listen too, and without any evidence to back it up, I want to say that the movies she blew into our minds with her magic-lantern words achieved their higher form, their highest, with everything else stripped away from them.

IN THE EARLY AUGHTS I saw Sophie, and so Ezra, a fair bit, at dinners, or parties of friends, or the parties thrown by the establishments that those friends now worked for. Then, about two years after 9/11, I moved to London for a job and lost touch with Sophie. She and Ezra were still together, and I remember hearing at some point that they'd gotten engaged, that there would eventually be a wedding at her family's house on Long Island. By then I'd stopped fantasizing about her, I suppose. By then it had seemed good and right: that those two, whose match was so fated and well built and symmetrical, should lead the way into the farther fields, into the seemingly still faraway fields of adulthood, where eventually we would be put out to the pasture of parenthood. But time passed, and no wedding invitation came, and then other people we knew went ahead and got married, and then babies started to be born, some even to the last people we ever expected to go nuclear-family, and then one year, back in New York for the holidays, catching up with the friends I still stayed in touch with there, I finally heard that Sophie and Ezra had broken up.

BY THE TIME I encountered her decades later in the camp, Sophie was already in bad shape. Malnourished, weak, tubercular, she moved only between her pallet and the crossroads—the makeshift center of camp where distributions happened and lines were formed. I was more mobile, searching out what I could find or use or trade or eat, working my connections among formal and informal associations, still strong enough to keep busy so that my mind skipped and skimmed on the surface of grief and didn't get sucked under. In my comings and goings through the camp I would pass the medical station, the hall with broken windows where weddings were still performed, the guy who cut hair and the one who hawked containers, and the handyman in a turban who worked in the shade of an archway, who would take a broken gas burner or heater and, with a little sideways nod of his head, would always say "Tomorrow is good" to the owner impatient to know when he or she could return for it. Sometimes parts of the camp became flooded, and when the water was gone, there would be impassable mud. But I would always come back again to check on Sophie, and bring to her what I could. It felt good to be useful, good to be able to make things a little bit easier for her. When she ceased being able to move at all, or no longer cared to, I would sit with her, dipping a rag in water and laying it on her feverish head, or just holding her hand, and sometimes when she was a little better she would look out into the middle distance with her gray-violet eyes and unspool for us a part of some movie. Once she did all of *E.T.*, from the opening when the alien spaceship lights blink through the silhouette of pine needles, and those two long, knobby, supra-prehensile brown fingers reach up and pluck down a branch for a better view, and you just know that one's not going to make it back on board in time, all the way until the crushing goodbye. When Sophie got to the end, this little elfin kid under a floppy hat with his arms wrapped around his knees started to weep, the tears making clean tracks down his dirty face until he windshield-wiped it all away with his hoodie sleeve.

A few times I managed to get her up, and we limped her out to the chain-link fence, beyond which you could see the barbed wire and the military trucks, but beyond still those a patch of listless gray sea. It reminded us that there were still beautiful places left. From there we couldn't smell the plastic people burned for warmth that hurt the lungs to inhale. Someone had dragged a busted easy chair out there, the fabric shredded and the crumbly yellow foam exploding through. But it was wide enough that both of us could get into it and sit shoulder to shoulder, and, looking out, we sometimes picked up this or that jumbled, unassembled thing that had happened to us all those years ago, and looked at it for a while without the hope of using it for anything or returning it to any rightful place. Not unrelatedly, there was a lot of trash blown up against the fence or lodged in its holes, plastic bottles and bags and so forth, and fifteen or twenty feet away from where we sat there was a large piece of torn black plastic that the wind had flung against the fence and arranged there in a shape that looked exactly like a coat. A long, wide-collared black coat with flowing folds that seemed to have been hung there as deliberately as one would hang it on a hook in the cozy entryway of a house, to wait until the owner was ready to go out again. So much did this piece of plastic sheeting resemble a coat that we watched first an old man and then a burly woman in a sailor's hat hurriedly approach it until each got close enough for the illusion to reveal itself as just a piece of trash.

That coat—Sophie said, after the woman had gone off, slumped and sheepish—it reminds me.

The wind was playing in the hem of the thing.

It happened, she told me, maybe six months before she and Ezra broke up. It was winter, and she was walking with a friend in Chelsea, looking at the galleries, maybe. They turned the corner onto the West Side Highway, and the icy wind off the Hudson came slicing into them. She started to shiver, and her friend, who lived abroad and whom she rarely saw, paused whatever he'd been in the middle of saying to ask if she wanted his coat. She said no, because of course she wasn't about to take the coat off his back, no matter how cold she was. And then the conversation continued, but almost without her. She stayed back, frozen in that question, amazed that he had asked it: that someone might think to ask such a thing so intuitively, as if thoughtfulness were so much part of his nature that the question, which housed such kindness, such genuine concern, could be nearly automatic. It was simply who he was, how he had been taught, or maybe taught himself, to live. And his care touched a nerve in her, because she'd begun to feel, more and more, that it was something the man she was living with, and with whom she planned to spend the rest of her life, lacked. It occurred to her that in all the years she'd been with him, Ezra had never once offered her his sweater or jacket. And I was almost always cold! she said. Always shivering, even when everyone else was warm. Though it's possible he didn't notice.

But it was more than that, she said. She could be sick in bed, and he wouldn't think to bring her a cup of tea, which wouldn't have cost him anything. Once, she was making him a bagel and the knife slipped and cut deeply into her thumb. She held it under the cold water, bleeding. He got up from the counter and came around to her, and she thought he was going to hug her from behind, but instead he picked up the knife and finished cutting the bagel, and put it in the toaster himself. It wasn't that he didn't love her, she said. She always knew that he loved her, in so far as he was capable. He was just busy, he was absorbed, he had no instinct for how to take care of someone else, which has to begin with noticing, with listening. But in that moment that her friend understood that she was cold and paused what he was saying to offer his own coat, she felt the pain of what she'd been missing.

The wind kept playing in Sophie's hair as she spoke, revealing the bald patches of her scalp.

It hadn't been the kind of thing she could have explained to anyone, she told me. In so many ways, she knew that she and Ezra had been lucky to have found each other. To enjoy each other as much as they did. Lucky to have found certain quiet rhythms of life, of closeness, that had sustained them. Anything she might have said about it to anyone else would have sounded ungrateful. Would have sounded like complaining, she'd thought, to friends who'd gone through rough breakups, or been treated badly, who'd had their hearts broken, or were alone because they couldn't find anyone.

Then one day they went to see a movie. It was in French, she said, and in some ways you could say that it was a very simple story. A story about the private life of an old couple, retired music teachers, who have been happy together for a very long time. They go to a concert, and the next morning, while they are eating breakfast in the kitchen in their robes, the wife suffers her first stroke. And from then on, the film remains there in those rooms of their conjoined inner life, trying to work out what happens when there is a couple who have been together for a lifetime, and one of them suddenly becomes an invalid. When it's up to the other to figure out how to care for her, to help her to live with the least amount of suffering and indignity.

Sophie had sat in the dark theater watching the face of the elderly husband, she told me. Watching his expression as he cared for his wife with such patience, such tenderness and loyalty. His wife had made him promise not to send her back to the hospital ever again, and he wouldn't break that promise, no matter what strain it put on him. He isn't a saint. He loses his temper, and once he even slaps his wife out of frustration that she refuses to eat or drink, that he is alone in trying to keep her alive. But never once does he fail to try, fail to care. It's continuous with who he has been to her, and what she has been to him, for more than fifty years. Though the fact that it's intuitive, an expression of his nature, doesn't mean that it doesn't tax him or require enormous effort.

Toward the end of the film, Sophie began to think of her own parents. Of how, despite the fact that they'd fought all their lives, they'd always taken care of each other. That they would continue to take care of each other until the very end was beyond question, and to some degree, Sophie told me, she had always lived in the shelter of that assumption, of what it meant not only about her parents but about love, about people in general. But now she understood that she herself had chosen differently. Other things had been important to her when she was younger, and as a result she'd chosen a man who—though he was many things to her—would never have the capacity to take care of her if she ceased to be able to take care of herself.

When the movie was over and they walked back outside into the sunlight, she knew then that something much bigger had ended. And not long after that, she told Ezra that it was over, that she couldn't marry him.

Sophie smiled a crooked half smile now, and looked out past the barbed wire to the smudged gray sea. Then she shrugged her bony shoulders and lifted her empty palms skyward, as if to gesture at the absurdity—though which aspect of it she was referring to, I couldn't say. The absurdity of believing that the decisions about who we love, and who we bind ourselves to, could ever be arrived at rationally? Or of assuming that we would be afforded a fair or natural death? Or did she mean the absurdity of having once believed in the possibility of dedicating one's life to anything beyond tomorrow, beyond just surviving? Or just the simple, long-standing absurdity of having lived a beginning that bore so little relation to the end?

I wasn't there when her end came. I was standing in line somewhere, or searching for a connection, or looking for water, or waiting.

In the Garden

For twenty-one years I was employed as the personal secretary to Latin America's greatest landscape architect, a man you almost certainly will have heard of. If you haven't heard of him, you will have sat in one of the parks he designed, unless you make it your business to avoid public places, in which case you might have been lucky enough to sit in one of the many private gardens he created, in our beautiful city or outside of it, in the hills or valleys, inland or by the sea. And if you were among the very luckiest, you might even have visited the garden he designed for himself on the estate of Three Winds, one of the most intriguing gardens in the world according to scholars and experts, on par with El Novillero and Compton Acres. If so, we've probably even met, since it was I who received guests in the role of personal secretary during my years at Three Winds, ushering the new arrival into the living room, always cool no matter how oppressive the heat outside, or, if he was staying overnight, to the guest room. There I would leave the guest in peace to collect himself after his travels, to change his clothes or rest in the rattan chair. Twenty minutes later I would knock again with a glass of lemonade on a beaten copper tray and the invitation to meet on the patio at half past, when Latin America's greatest landscape architect would begin his personal tour of the acres brimming with rare species, so rare you would have to walk into the heart of the forest for days to find them, and perhaps even then you might not.

Some of the trees he planted over half a century ago. When I die, he used to say, remember not to move anything. Not even the pills on the night table? I would ask. All right, he used to say, but only the pills. I'm a realist and a man of the earth! he used to shout when I looked at him the wrong way. I built my house with my own hands, so I don't think it's too much to ask that when I die, my glasses be left where I put them down! Because it was his hope (now trampled by history, into whose path he stumbled) that Three Winds would become a museum where the public would come and fall in love with the flora of our beautiful country, as he had. He carried his burden of regrets the same as anyone—so many of his dreams never came to fruition, and others only after many compromises—but on those acres, at least, everything existed according to his design, as far as was possible: the rest was up to nature.

And nature, as he used to say, is not a peaceful thing. It's not a gentle breeze and the sun coming up over the mountains, as they'd have you believe in children's books. It's not little pink buds or a rhapsody in green. (Have you ever noticed that what passes for green in this country is really black? An infinity of black leaves?) Nature is a cruel and conniving affair, he used to say to me when we were alone together, which was often. It's aggressive, and surprisingly fatal. The weak are killed, first tormented and then killed, and the strong are nourished by the rot and decay. So don't let them talk to you about how peaceful it all is, the wind in the trees and the sound of the crickets. The crickets are alone; they drag their wings across a vein out of which teeth grow, in the hope that another of their kind will find them, either to mate or to fight. Don't let them talk to you about the sound of the crickets, or quote you poems about roses. I'm not saying flowers shouldn't be picked and enjoyed for their beauty, I'm only saying that your picking and enjoying are part of their plan, not vice versa.

Not that he always talked like that. After a good meal in the presence of friends, he could carry on for hours about the prehistoric ginkgo that holds the knowledge of dinosaurs, the bromeliads that survive on motes of dust and droplets of humidity, or the moss garden of Saihoji, whose pond is covered by a skin of algae through which the rain falls peaceably to its death. He could philosophize about the garden of Epicurus, or captivate with stories of his adventures into the rain forest, or his youthful travels in Asia, where he'd followed the trail of Basho as far as Haguro. It all depended on his mood, which could be overturned like a bottle of ink, sending the blackness spilling. In the final years, there were no longer many friends left. But at the beginning they came from all over the world, famous writers, artists, dignitaries of all kinds, to receive a private tour of Three Winds and sign the gold-tasseled visitors' book.

FOR TWENTY-ONE YEARS I served as personal secretary to Latin America's greatest landscape architect. They were dark years in our country's history, but outside the sun shone, as it has always shone here, and always will. Behind closed doors, in basements, in warehouses, in secret complexes, the sun did not shine, but outside it shone always. A garden depends on sun. A garden is an arrangement of light, he used to say, one has to think how the sun will set on it, how it will rise, from which direction it will shine, how it will pass through; how every leaf will reveal or obscure.

On the day I graduated from the Horticultural Institute, the sun was shining as usual, and I rode my bicycle to the new park in the north of the city, the one already made famous by the newspapers, though construction had only just begun. I presented myself at the park office. At the time it was temporarily housed in a building that later became a café where visitors could order coffee and sit outside in the shade of a giant plane tree. (The tree itself hadn't arrived yet on a flatbed truck; it was still bending in the provincial wind somewhere, oblivious of the plans in store for it.) There he was, sitting behind a desk piled with papers and drawings, the famous botanist and landscape architect, newly crowned director of public gardens, browned and silvered from sun and age. He hardly glanced at me. I'd like to apply for a job, I announced. We have all the gardeners we need, he said, and went on turning the pages. I don't know what possessed me—maybe the courage that comes with being in the presence of one's fate—but I said: You don't have one like me.

Now he looked up, and a species of smile slid across his face, then disappeared around the back of his head. He studied my pants first, the dirt under my nails, and at last my face. I stiffened under his gaze. And what sort is that? he asked, leaning back so that his chair was forced to let out a terrified squeal. I thought of the withered *Phalaenopsis bellina* I'd found in the garbage a few months earlier, which I brought home and tended until one day it began to send out green shoots again, and, God help me, I said: The kind that can wring new life out of the dead.

The park was still under construction: the paths weren't yet laid, the future greenhouse was just a pit of tepid water filled with mosquito larvae, they were only beginning to haul in the dirt for the rolling hills of the upper gardens, and the busts of the generals were still being forged at the official foundry. But he must have sensed how fully I understood the beauty of what he intended, a wildness barely contained. He must have sensed, too, my willingness, the wholehearted way I was prepared to throw myself into the work. I had no other loyalties: no parents, no children, no ambition other than to exist among leaves and Latin names. That first day I sat beside him taking notes he dictated to me as he paged through the plans, and I didn't miss a thing, didn't need to be told how to spell *Trochodendron aral-ioides* or *Xanthorrhoea preissii*, and when on occasion he mistook one plant for its cousin I made the correction without drawing attention to the mistake. At four he dismissed me and told me to return with clean nails the following day. At eight o'clock sharp I took up my place again by his side. I had only the great-est respect for him. I felt that I had been—what was it? That I had been chosen, above all. Without being told, I knew when to shadow him and when to make myself scarce, when to provide the word he was looking for and when to absorb his words like a heavy rain.

WHAT DO YOU want me to say? he used to shout. I'm a realist and a man of the earth, both of which require few words! If I hadn't become what I became, I might have become a poet. I respect them enormously, the poets, he used to say. We each have to work with what we have, I with the once rich flora of our country, so much of which is now teetering on the brink of extinction, and they with our language, which is suffering the same fate. When I was a boy there were many more words, he'd say, but one by one they've fallen out of use. History has reached the point where language is sliding backward; one day we will be restored to speechlessness, and then, as if to prove the point, he'd go sit on the veranda and collect from the garden a gloomy silence. But he never managed to remain silent for long. Sooner or later, the words still left would burst out of him.

Neither of us came from this country. He was more from it than I, having been born in the capital, but his mother was born in the Carpathian Mountains and his father in Leipzig, and he grew up in the abandoned zones between world-class languages, which is perhaps why he gravitated to one that, however dead, offered a proper name for everything. And, being dead, it never changes. A lake is a lake is a lake forever. A lake cannot one day become a blind eye or a grave.

ONE AFTERNOON, AS we were inspecting a new shipment of ferns and orchids in the upper gardens, a procession of three black sedans with darkened windows drove up the alley of imperial palms, unsettling a cloud of dust, and halted in front of the temporary park office. The sight of them, like dark weasels among the greenery, sent chills up my spine. All four doors of the first car sprung open, and four men in military uniforms and gold sunglasses got out. One of them rapped on the door of the park office, entered, and after some moments emerged again. Then all four doors of the second car opened, and four more men in uniform emerged, one of whom gestured leisurely in our direction. The doors of the third black sedan remained closed. Shouldn't you go to them? I asked. Yes, he said, but remained glued to the spot, a small *Aphelandra squarrosa* trembling in his palm. Yes of course, he said again, more to the plant than to anyone else. In the end, they came and got him and took him away in the third black sedan. A single door was opened from within, and I remember that as he stood peering into the dark upholstered interior, the look on his face was that of a man standing on the edge of an abyss, equally afraid of falling and of throwing himself in.

Plan by plan, sketch by sketch, undulating bed by bed, he bent the neck of nature. Nature isn't a daisy chain, it isn't a pocketful of posies, he used to say. Nature bites the hand that feeds it. But he never tried to tame nature, he never removed its claws or its venom. That was his secret, what set him apart from the rest: he only bent nature's neck, he never broke it. That was his genius and his downfall, too. He let nature keep its wildness, and one day nature turned around and struck him down. Not one day, in fact—very slowly, stealthily, but the result was the same.

I watched the procession of cars disappear the same way they had come, and then, however shaken, I went back to my work—my work, after all, which was no more and no less than dutifully tending to the frail and exhausted plants that had journeyed from far and wide to take their place in the illustrious park, designed by the great botanist and landscape architect who had taught people to see exquisite beauty in the native species of his country. That night, a bright blue spring night, I rode home on my bicycle and took a bath and watched the dirt swirl away down the drain, where it would join all of the other sediment making its slow way back to the sea, floating down league after soundless league. I wanted to call someone to tell them what had taken place, but who was there to call? I thought it was possible that I might never see him again, which, looking back, shows just how naive I was about the way the generals worked.

That night I didn't sleep. The following day, when I arrived early at the park, he was already sitting behind his desk. He looked terrible; either he'd slept in his clothes or he hadn't slept at all. But I was relieved all the same. I boiled the water for tea. When I brought in the tray, he insisted on pouring the steaming liquid for both of us. His hand shook ever so slightly, and the tea splashed into the saucer. There are things you should know, he said quietly. Should I? I asked, and dropped a heaping spoonful of sugar into his cup. I stirred, and we watched the sugar dissolve. These are not ordinary times, he whispered. To build a park like this, one has to sleep with the devil. I folded my hands in my lap, the hands of a simple gardener, and studied my nails. A garden is an arrangement of light. One has to think from which direction the sun will shine, how it will set and how it will rise, which leaf will reveal and which will obscure. I unrolled the plans for the park, and wordlessly—yes, with a trace of my finger—I drew his attention to this or that detail, until his vision returned to him. Then I stood and put the tea things away. God dwells in your gardens, I said, and walked out the door to begin the morning's work.

HE INVITED ME to Three Winds. It was an invitation that could mean many things, and only as I felt my stomach tighten did I realize that I had been waiting for it. The estate was more than an hour away by car, on the coastal plain. I rode up front with his driver while he rode in the back seat, and from time to time I felt his eyes resting on the back of my neck, very lightly, like a fly. Three Winds was a garden turned inward. It was there that he cultivated himself; there that he experimented most wildly, without restraint. When he gave me a tour of the grounds, I remember the shock I felt coming upon the concrete walls with no roof, like a ruin from the future, or the shiny, damp path that wound through the undergrowth to a cathedral of trees. Afterward he led me to the nursery, the tropical plant collection, the herbarium, to the little Benedictine chapel dedicated to Saint Francis, and finally to his painting studio, engulfed by vines. As I stood before one of his large canvases, a riot of interlocking colors, I felt a hand glide heavily to my shoulder. His breath was warm and heavy, and he smelled of sandalwood and wine. What do you see? he said close to my ear. It's a fine painting, sir, I told him. I heard a gurgle in the back of his throat. Perhaps you aren't the man I thought you were, he whispered. I see a precipice in front, and wolves behind, I said. His fingers tightened their grip on my shoulder. You do, don't you? he said. You do?

Not long after that, my things were sent for and the small room next to the kitchen that faced east was given to me as my own. The bed was narrow but comfortable, and from the chair I had a view of a cherry tree, whose fruit got riper by the day. On the windowsill I set the little pewter box from where I was born, with the views of Henkersteg, the Opera House, and Bratwurst Glöcklein, and on the shelf I arranged my botany books. I quickly took up my new duties. I answered letters, oversaw the orders, arranged the schedule, supervised the staff, and saw to the needs, great and small, of Latin America's greatest landscape architect. His work was never done, but sometimes there were quiet moments together, too, and I don't think it's too much to say that then he was the happiest I ever saw him.

That time didn't last. When we are given fair warning, does what happens next not always seem inevitable? When the generals came from the city and arrived at Three Winds in their dark cars, I met them at the top of the drive, brought them to the house, and served them glasses of lemonade on the beaten copper tray. We stood on ceremony. They toured the grounds. In the little chapel of Saint Francis, one of them got down on his knees and crossed himself. When they were getting ready to leave, the same general couldn't find his sunglasses, and the landscape architect fell to the floor and began crawling frantically among the chairs of the long dining table. I'd never seen him like that, like a dog or a cockroach, and I wanted to shout at him to get up, but at the same time I knew there was no choice but to join him. At that moment I remembered the chapel. I ran back to it, and sure enough there were the sunglasses, glinting under the empty pew. The general examined them to make sure they were intact, and then he smiled at me and slowly rubbed away my fingerprints with a handkerchief.

And soon afterward, very soon after that, the lower gardens in the heart of the public park in the city were replaced on the plans by a shimmering lake, a lake so deep that no one could reach the bottom, which anyway was concrete. The bulldozers rolled in to tear up the ground, wildly scooping up shrubs, and the dark loam was carted away in trucks that rumbled up and down the alley of imperial palms. Four days passed, during which the hole gaped under the blank sky. At last they came one night, the people who are in the business of what lies at the bottom. They buried what the generals wished to bury, then they poured the concrete. If there was gunfire, or screams, or if there was only the silence of the dead, I don't know. We were far away, cloistered in Three Winds, where the grandfather clock from Leipzig gently ticked off the hours. It must have taken a small army of them, with their trucks and floodlights, because in the morning the concrete had already dried in the sun that never ceases to shine. A few weeks later the lake was filled, the sun busied itself on the blue surface, and an official message came from the Supreme Chief of the Nation himself: paddleboats. That was all. The birds arrived on their own, as soon as the duckweed and water lilies were laid in.

From my room I could hear him call to me no matter where he was in the house, though in time I learned to recognize the sounds that preceded a question, and before he could even ask,

I was there in the doorway. If the telephone rang, it was I who answered it; I who knew whether he was able to talk just then, or whether a message needed to be taken; I who instructed the cook on what was to be prepared for dinner, who helped him to bed when he drank too much, who brought him the first steaming cup of tea in the morning, in the sixteenth-century bowl sent to him by an admirer in Japan; I who handed him his pencil, his hat, his stick, his trowel, his knife; I who came with the first aid kit whenever he cut himself, because he was— our greatest landscape architect and botanist—squeamish at the sight of his own blood.

THINGS GROW IN this country, under a sun like this. Under the watchful eye of the generals' bronze gaze, the imperial palms grew. The giant lily pads grew as large as tables. The giant bamboo grew until it was four or five stories high, and when the breeze blew through it the stalks made a clacking sound, and as they leaned in the wind, they creaked like the sound of braking streetcars, and somehow there was also the sound of horses' hooves and a braying donkey, even a whole barnyard of animals, contained in that bamboo. There were whispers, and the sound of children playing, or maybe crying, or just singing softly. But Latin America's greatest landscape architect never heard them, because after construction was complete, and the opening ceremony attended, he had no time to return to the parks and gardens he'd designed during his tenure as director of public gardens—parks, after all, that were visited and enjoyed by the many who came to walk their paths or rest on their benches. Those were busy years for him. I won't lie: they were mostly

good years, too. He had his work. The grotesque incident of the
lake was never repeated. And when, after almost fifteen years,
some of the generals fled the country, and a few were put on
trial, and most retreated behind the tall stucco walls of their
mansions to live out the rest of their lives in the peace of their
own gardens, no one bothered with our country's landscape
architect; he, too, was left in peace.

What do you want me to say? he used to shout. My work was
straightforward: I collected plants and designed parks and gardens. No more and no less. I live in a house I built with my own
hands, surrounded by my acres of plants and trees, some common and some very rare, so rare you would have to walk into
the heart of the forest for days, as I did, to find them. Some of
the trees I planted long ago, when I was young, he would shout,
and now they are old, like me, and yet, unlike me, their plans
haven't been ruined, sullied and ruined, suffocated in darkness.
Once—only once—did I look him squarely in the eye and say,
quietly and clearly: It isn't you who got suffocated in darkness.
I'll never forget the look on his face, like a child who had never
before been slapped across the mouth. He recoiled, or tried to
recoil, but in the end one can't recoil from oneself.

IN THE LAST years we used to travel, which was the only
thing that gave temporary relief to his moods. We went to the
Alhambra. In Lake Como, we stayed at the Villa d'Este and
walked through the gardens of the Villa Carlotta and the Villa
Cipressi. We went to Arezzo to see the Piero della Francescas,
and to Florence to see the Fra Angelicos. It was my first time
in Italy, and he insisted that I climb the stairs to the top of

the Duomo and tour its double shell, while he sat having coffee below. At a time agreed upon in advance, I was to exit onto the tiny lookout terrace at the very top and wave to him, and he, in turn, was to wave back at me. The going was difficult—the stairs were steep, and the passageways were very narrow, and many times I had to beat back a suffocating sense of claustrophobia. I had to run up the last flights of stairs to make it to the lookout to wave at the appointed time, and when I got there, I was gasping for breath. The claustrophobia turned out to be nothing compared with the vertigo. Gripping the wall, legs shaking, I looked down over the ledge. Far below, among the little white specks of the café tables set out on the square, I saw a figure waving. I waved back. He waved again, and I waved once more. He went on waving, as if out of inertia. How long must this go on? I wondered. And then I understood that I was considering leaving him—leaving him alone with all of those ghosts and demons and starting life again, somewhere else. Everything was still possible for me, the door stood open. Down below, he continued waving. Now I had the feeling that he was trying to say something. Don't ask me how I knew; obviously I couldn't make out his face from so high up. Somehow I just knew that he was mouthing something to me, or maybe shouting it, both of which were equally futile. I thought that something was wrong, so I turned and hurried all the way down the narrow stairs, going around and around and still not reaching the bottom, getting nowhere near the bottom, frankly, while, God knows, he might have been having a heart attack in the square. But when I finally emerged into the daylight and ran to the café, sweating profusely, I found him absorbed in a newspaper.

What were you trying to tell me? I asked. Tell you? he said. What do you mean? I was blinded by the glare. I didn't even know whether you were up there.

I'm not a Christian, but many times I found myself drawn into the chapel at Three Winds, to look again at the small painting of Saint Francis holding the dove. There are those who committed terrible crimes. And there are those who acquiesced. What I never knew was, what is it to acquiesce to the acquiescent? Sometimes a long time would pass as I stood there, so long that the fingers of colored sun that fell through the stained glass would shift to a different wall. No, not just to yield but, in one's own way, to affirm?

Our last trip was to America. It was winter there, and I took his father's fur coat out of storage, the Russian sable that he had brought with him from Leipzig. It smelled of the cedar trunk, but it was still beautiful. Wrapped in that fur that almost touched the floor, he was something strangely impressive, and people turned to look as he passed. The coat made him talk more loudly, as if he couldn't hear himself in it, which drew even more attention. He refused to take it off, even indoors, and sometimes, as he was eating in the hotel's grand breakfast room, a little bit of food would fall into the fur and lodge there, food that I would later try to brush off when he wasn't looking, or when he had fallen asleep in the back of the taxi after a long day of walking. At those times, I saw how old he was getting, and a panic would come over me. How could I keep everything in its proper place? Shoes under the bed. Glass on the table. Dove in the hand. Chair by the door. Trowel at the ready. Cook in the kitchen. Sun in the sky. Leaf on the ground. Light on the lake.

It was too much, like one of those dreams where every time you turn, something else has moved behind your back. But he would always wake up, and, still sunk in that enormous fur, he would begin to talk again (to himself or to me, I never really knew), and I would go back to listening as usual, nodding now and then but otherwise not saying much, close to nothing at all, and everything was exactly as it had been between us, as it always would be.

The Husband

I
—

On a freezing gray winter ghetto of a day in March, her mother calls to say that the lost Husband has arrived. She doesn't begin the conversation that way, of course. She begins casually enough, the way stories so often begin, stories of everyday life onto which is sprung a sudden intrusion: *The other day the doorbell rang, though I wasn't expecting anyone.*

Tamar is eating lunch in the West Seventy-Eighth Street office where she sees patients, but in Tel Aviv it is already evening. Her mother still lives there, in the same apartment where Tamar and her brother grew up, on Tchernichovsky Street, behind Gan Meir, whose trees can be seen through the large, dirty windows.

Who is it? her mother shouted into the receiver. But when she pressed the button to listen, no one was there.

Tamar spears a pineapple chunk and settles in for the story, just like she has for countless of her mother's stories over the years: often long, usually funny or absurd, sometimes rudderless tales whose only point was to keep Tamar attached to the distant life of her family. Looking out at a slice of the sky that had been dumping slush on the city all morning, she sees the old door of the family apartment with its peeling brown laminate chipped at the bottom edge, and the plastic intercom covered in fingerprints inky from the newspaper, and is filled with a pleasant warmth.

I thought someone had pressed the wrong buzzer, her mother tells her, it happens all the time. When the baby upstairs was born, they pushed my buzzer like the flusher of the only toilet in a crowded bus station. But eventually everyone left, and since then it's been quiet except for the sound of the baby screaming. The parents do their best, her mother said, but sometimes they shout at each other. They used to be so happy, so in love, but since the baby was born, they can't agree on anything.

Sounds familiar, says Tamar, since she and the children's father had stopped agreeing not long after their difficult first baby was born, though they'd hung on for nine or ten years before finally separating. After that, both Tamar and her mother had been single, her father having died a year earlier of a heart attack. There had been four of them in the family—her mother, her father, her younger brother, and Tamar—and for a long time three of them had been married, and only her brother remained unmarried. Then their father died, Tamar got divorced, and Shlomi married his boyfriend, making him the only one with a husband.

Her mother buzzed down to ask who was there, but when she pushed the button to listen, there was only the sound of a car driving past, of night in the city, a humid one by the sea. She went back to the kitchen, filled the kettle, and set it on the stove, but a minute later the buzzer sounded again. This time she ignored it, but it started up more impatiently: a few quick bursts and then a long angry buzz. All right, all right, her mother shouted. Who is it? And once more she pressed the button to listen.

Special services, a man said.

So that's the way they get in to rape old women nowadays, her mother thought.

No, thank you, she said into the intercom, I don't want any special services.

Social Services, the man shouted back.

Thank you but no, she said, because what's the difference, really?

Mrs. Paz? Ilana Paz? It's Ron Azrak from Social Services here. Can you please buzz us in?

What do you want? her mother asked, but forgot to press the button to talk and was apparently still listening, so that she heard him softly say: Perhaps you'd like to talk to her yourself?

She jabbed the button again: Who's with you?

That's what I want to talk to you about, the man said.

He had a kind voice, her mother explains to Tamar, not the voice of a murderer or a rapist.

What's it about? her mother demanded.

Mrs. Paz, it really would be better for everyone if we could come up to talk in person—

Give me a synopsis, she interrupted.

Special Services replied that it was a sensitive matter, and if she would just open the door for them, he'd be happy to give her his card. Tamar's mother considered telling him to go away, but curiosity got the better of her and she gave in. But before buzzing him in she turned off the stove (Tamar knows she would never leave the apartment with the stove on for even a moment, someone she knew as a girl had burned to death that way), climbed the stairs, and knocked on the door of the couple with the baby. The husband answered with a stained burp cloth over his shoulder. He looks terrible, Tamar's mother tells her; since the birth, his eczema has flared up.

I'm sorry to bother you, Tamar's mother said to him, but someone is outside claiming to be from Special Services. In case it happens that I buzz in a thug or a lowlife, would you mind keeping your door open and listening out? If our own thug of a building manager would install a security camera, none of this would be necessary, but hell will melt over before that happens, apologies again for bothering you, especially with the baby, such a sweet child, it's a joy to see how your family is blossoming, all right then, thank you, if you really don't mind, I'll go and buzz him in, no, no need to come down with me, just stay right where you are but with the door open just like that so you can hear me if I scream.

Back in her apartment, she called down to the entryway.

All right, I'm buzzing you in. Come through the first door, then wait in the entryway until it closes all the way behind you, then I'll buzz a second time to open the inner door.

It's like getting into the vaults of Bank Leumi, he said.

But with no money inside, her mother replied, to nip that idea in the bud.

She waited, watching through the peephole until two blurry figures appeared, a tall man carrying a briefcase and a little old one wearing a hat. The tall one took out a handkerchief.

Tamar imagines them: the little one with a brown felt hat, and the tall one whose forehead has begun to glisten with sweat, a high forehead, the hairline receded considerably, by next year he'll be bald, but with a nice curly black beard, and delicate glasses. She sees her mother opening the door a crack without unhooking the chain that Tamar installed four or five years ago, just before she returned to New York and installed an alarm system in her own house, since she, too, was newly on her own.

Social Services slid his business card through the opening.

Thank you, I apologize for the trouble. Ron Azrak. May we come in?

What kind of name is Azrak?

He smiled. He had a nice face, her mother tells her, very warm eyes.

Turkish, my grandfather was born in Istanbul.

Really? I've always wanted to go to Turkey.

There's still time, Social Services said with a sparkle in his eyes, knowing just what to say to make an old woman feel good, somewhere there was a mother proud to have raised a son like him, so polite and considerate, so what if there's no PhD after his name, her mother tells her, out of the kindness of his heart and a sense of duty to his people he's chosen to work in Special Services, a thankless job if ever there was one.

You mean Social Services, Tamar says, tossing the rest of

her lunch into the trash and glancing at the clock: still twenty minutes before her next patient.

Right, says her mother.

The Bosphorus! her mother had probably said to Social Services, showing off the knowledge she'd absorbed from countless hours of late-night TV. If there's a river in the world with a better name, I don't know it. And to think that it divides two continents! she'd have said, because her mother also knew how to turn on the charm if she wanted to.

I'd like to explain why I'm here, Ilana, said Social Services. I think you should sit down, it all may come as a bit of a shock.

He led her to the sofa. She hadn't exactly invited him in, her mother tells her, give an inch and they take a foot.

I didn't expect you to recognize him right away, it's been so many years. Social Services glanced back at the door, and again her mother caught sight of the old man in a hat and dark suit, standing mutely in the hallway. We just found him a few days ago, he's still a little out of sorts, Social Services said. Do you recognize him?

I thought he was your sidekick, her mother said, shifting uncomfortably on the sofa and trying to remember if there was someone to whom she owed money. Social Services laughed, showing his big Turkish teeth.

Now, he said, suddenly serious. Since you asked about my family, would you allow me to tell you a little story?

Her mother looked at the clock and was dismayed to discover that it wasn't yet eight thirty. It had been years since she'd fallen asleep before midnight. But I thought to myself, the television can wait, she tells Tamar. Who am I to turn away such a polite Scheherazade?

All right, she said, trying to ignore the old man that someone spilled at her front door like a puddle.

Social Services took out his handkerchief, and once more blotted his forehead.

Shall I open the window for some air? her mother asked.

Why not?

Because someone with a knife might come through it.

What?

A little breeze would do me a world of good, too, but I live by myself, Mr. Azrak, my daughter lives in New York, and my son is a long story.

Call me Ron.

I live by myself, Ron, and I'm no longer young, as you can see, so I have to be cautious.

Tamar imagines the warm air wafting in, carrying the sound of a moped and a couple arguing as they pass on the street below, and Social Services beckoning to the old man still standing at the door, who, without removing his hat, enters, walking slowly, until a few feet in front of her mother he stops, and with a calm and unreadable expression studies her hair dyed copper, her broad face with its freckled cheeks, still surprisingly smooth, her sharp brown eyes, her T-shirt that says "Trust Me, I'm a Doctor." Tamar imagines how suddenly her mother wishes she'd worn something that might have made a better impression, because it has been a long time since anyone looked at her with such care. How she gestures to a chair, trying to ignore the skin prickling at the back of her neck, and how he takes off his hat and holds it to his chest and takes a seat by the open window, sitting upright as if waiting for the plane to take off before daring to recline. How her mother puts the kettle back on the stove, and when she returns Social Services is also peering at her curiously through his silver-rimmed glasses, since when did she become so interesting to everyone?

And then, her mother continues, Social Services launches into a story about his grandparents. Not the Turkish ones, the ones on the other side, his mother's parents, who came from Salonica.

An international family, Tamar says.

But all from the same small corner of the world. When his father met his mother, he was delighted to learn that she already knew how to cook all his favorite dishes.

Tamar waits for her mother, who has been off the hook of having to cook for anyone since Tamar's father died, to say something snide about this, but she doesn't. Instead she recounts the story Social Services told her, about how his grandparents met as teenagers in Salonica, though it took time for his grandfather to convince his grandmother to love him. How they finally married in 1939, and moved into a small apartment together outside the old walls of the city, and his grandfather began to work in the dry goods store that had been in his grandmother's family for two hundred years. As he spoke, her mother could practically smell the Aegean lapping in the old port and the fuel of the ships, and could hear the doves cooing in the quiet street where the couple lived. Behind her, the dark puddle also listened, the room was quiet, even Tchernichovsky Street was quiet while Mussolini's bombs fell on Salonica. But she couldn't relax with those eyes resting on the back of her neck.

My grandparents lost each other during the war, Social Services told her. Each made it to Israel, each was told that the other was dead, and neither could bear to return to Salonica, where fifty thousand were deported and almost no one survived. And then one day, two weeks before my grandmother was supposed to get remarried to an older man, also a widower from the war, my grandfather saw her in the window of a bus passing in front of him on Allenby Street.

There was a moment of silence in the room. How extraordinary, her mother finally said, what a story! But now I really must ask what your business is here. Surely Social Services has better things to do than send storytellers to pay house calls on elderly women.

Yes, of course, he said with a gentle laugh, I was only telling it because it happens more often than you think. The lost are found, couples and siblings reunited, and, well, as you'll see— have you really not guessed already? Of course, it's a perfectly natural response, we can take things as slowly as you'd like.

Take what? her mother demanded, and by now she really was beginning to feel irritated, she tells Tamar. I have no idea what you're talking about, will you please explain exactly why you're here?

At that moment Ron Azrak got up, straightened the pleats of his khaki pants, cleared his throat, came to her side, and with a gentle smile, laid his hand on her arm.

You see, he said, gesturing to the wrinkled old man sitting by the window, we've found him at last.

Who? her mother asked, pulling her arm away and patting her head for her reading glasses.

You must have given up hope.

Hope? For what? she demanded, not bothering to hide her growing aggravation.

Your husband, he whispered, his eyes fluttering lightly as if to protect themselves from violence.

My husband? she nearly bellowed. What about him? To which Social Services, who must have been used to the frustration elicited by the ways and means of his agency, replied:

Here he is.

Laughter shoots from Tamar's mouth as her mother delivers this line. Her mother had also laughed, she tells Tamar, she laughed so loudly that it must have sounded like a scream, because suddenly the husband—not the one sitting by the window, and not the one who has been dead five years, but the one from upstairs—burst through the door, cradling the baby with her red, grimacing face.

What's going on here? he shouted, looking from the curly-haired Turk to the old man to her mother. She tried to explain, but every time she opened her mouth to speak, she collapsed back into peals of laughter. The baby spiked the air with a balled fist and let out a shriek. The husband from upstairs began to jiggle her, and when that didn't work, he began to bounce from foot to foot, still waiting to know whether his help was needed.

It's okay, her mother finally managed to get the words out, dabbing her eyes with a crumpled tissue from her pocket. There's been a misunderstanding, that's all! This man has confused me with someone else.

Hearing this, Social Services didn't balk, only offered an-other of his calm and pleasant agency smiles.

I assure you we haven't confused you with anyone.

Oh, but you have, Mr. Azrak, her mother said.

Ron, he insisted.

I'm sorry you've had to waste your time on me, her mother said, but my husband isn't missing at all. I know exactly where he is: buried in Yarkon Cemetery, next to his mother.

The husband from upstairs looked wide-eyed from her mother to Social Services, who wiped his palms on his pants, snapped open the brass latches of his briefcase, and removed a thick file. Through all of this, the old man continued to sit silently under his hat, rubbing his thumb and forefinger as if in the universal symbol for money. In the short time that he had been there, her mother observed, he seemed to have shrunk just the slightest bit.

The kettle now let out a shrieking whistle from the kitchen. Social Services turned expectantly to the husband from upstairs, who raised his eyebrows as if to say, Me? then frantically looked around for a place to put the miserable baby. At that moment the old man by the window opened his arms wide, as if to accept the baby, and the husband, so startled by the gesture and, frankly, by the whole scene, handed her over and hurried off to deal with the screaming kettle. As soon as the old man began to bounce the baby on his knee, she became quiet, and her eyes widened in wonder. His lips began to move, and a moment later, when the kettle suddenly went silent as well, the only sound in the apart-ment was the first sounds that came from the Husband's mouth, a quiet, wordless song that went: *Lyla ly, lyla ly la la la ly.*

And that is as far as her mother gets with her story, because now Tamar's own buzzer rings, and she tells her mother to hold while she lifts the receiver to ask who is there, and pushes the button that allows her patient to enter the lobby. As she does, juggling between her cell-phone headset and the ancient receiver connected to the door buzzer in the office, she could swear she hears her mother say, very quietly, The chicken will be ready in twenty minutes.

What? says Tamar.

Nothing, says her mother.

She tells her mother she'll call her back.

2

But the next time she speaks to her mother is not until the following day, because she doesn't pick up when Tamar tries her on the train back to Riverdale. This comes as a surprise: her mother has always picked up. It is already midnight in Tel Aviv, but her mother never goes to bed any earlier, which has always made the time difference between them less of an obstacle to keeping in close touch. Over the nineteen years that Tamar has lived in New York, she's gotten used to those late-afternoon/late-night conversations three or even four times a week, conversations during which she had at least eighty-five percent of her mother's attention, the rest remaining available to the wonders and trials being broadcast on her mother's TV. Sometimes her mother would interrupt their conversation to tell Tamar some fabulous fact about the Bengali tigers or the Alhambra, or to inform her of the struggles of children living in the slums of Beirut, or that an island in Greece was the place in the world whose inhabitants live the longest. If these conversations comforted Tamar, it was in part because they went all the way back to her childhood, to the privileged hours she used to spend in her mother's presence while her brother napped, basking in her attention, which seemed only marginally taken up by the pile of elementary-school tests in her lap that she corrected with a red pen.

When her mother doesn't pick up, Tamar calls Shlomi. She isn't worried, not really, but because worry has always been the currency of love in her family, rarely does anyone miss an opportunity to express it. Of the four of them, when there were still four, only Shlomi was relatively free of the habit, probably because their parents spent so many years worrying about him that he developed an allergy to it.

Shlomi is a night person like her mother, though only since he met Dan can he be found home at midnight. For the twenty or so years before that, Shlomi was out from nine p.m. until two or three in the morning, though it was often impossible to know when those hours fell for him, since his work as a DJ took him all over the world. But now that he has settled down and gotten married, he travels much less, and soon, once the surrogate expecting their baby in Nepal delivers, he will not be traveling at all. But Shlomi's circadian rhythms, fixed from his teenage years or maybe much earlier, come through to him from their mother's milk, can't be reset, which means that he picks up after two rings, using the nickname he's called her since they were little: What's up, Tash?

She launches right into the story about their mother, but he cuts her off to say that he knows all about it, and that this guy, the Husband, seems quite nice, very refined, not to mention excellent with children.

It is then that she feels the first pang of bewilderment— bewilderment mixed with annoyance. What do you mean, you know all about him? she asks. He stayed? The Husband? That's how you're referring to a stranger that Social Services scraped up from God knows where, from the bottom of some barrel?

From Netanya, in fact, Shlomi says, but she ignores him and continues.

The *Husband*? And Mom! She had me on the phone for half an hour and didn't even mention the fact that she's accepted into her life a man that someone she doesn't know from Adam showed up at her door and told her belongs to her? The way she told it made it sound like she thought the whole thing was crazy.

To which her brother replies: Maybe she felt uneasy telling you the truth.

It feels like a slap in the face. There is no malice in it, that isn't Shlomi's way, but, following from his freedom from worry, he has a talent for frankness.

Why would she be uneasy? asks Tamar, still stinging.

She can almost hear her brother shrug on the other end.

Because she knew you'd react like this.

Like what?

Prickly. Suspicious. A little defensive, even.

Defensive! Why would I be defensive? My response to a stranger being presented as her lost husband, when we all know that she never had any husband except for Dad, seems like the only sane reaction around here. What possessed her to take him in just like that, a perfect stranger?

Maybe because of that.

What?

That he seems perfect.

We don't even know the first thing about him, Shlomi! He might be a psychopath. Or at the very least a con artist.

Maybe she knows enough.

I mean, does he even speak Hebrew?

It sounded to Tamar as if they'd found him far away, maybe even at sea. An image comes to her of the old man in the brown hat clinging to a broken plank and bobbing in the waves. For a moment, she almost feels sorry for him. But only a moment, because, also, who does he think he is? Going along with Social Service's crazy idea, or maybe even cooking it up himself; sitting there in his dapper suit on her mother's chair like the picture of innocence itself, opening his arms to accept babies?

He speaks it like a poet, Shlomi says. Like he stepped right out of an Alterman poem, the kind Mom used to read us when we were young.

Now he's stepping out of Alterman poems!

And he's some sort of genius mathematician, too, Shlomi added. Collaborated with Erdős himself. The guy has an Erdős number of one.

Who the heck is Erdős? Tamar asks.

But Shlomi has to hang up, because, lo and behold, Dan has finally gotten through to Nepal.

3

That night Tamar doesn't sleep well. It's Friday, her daughter Iris is out late with friends, and on such nights Remy, only ten, likes to sleep in his mother's bed. She can never fall asleep until Iris is safely at home, and as much as she likes Remy's sweet presence, he's a mouth breather, and his hot skinny legs are always shifting under the sheets. Yet even after Iris is back in her own bed, not smelling of alcohol or cigarettes or weed, under the glowing sticker stars on her ceiling, and Remy has at last fallen into a place of stillness in the well of sleep, Tamar lies awake thinking about the Husband. What bothers her, she decides, is the idea of her mother being taken advantage of. As tough and sassy as she may be, she is still a seventy-three-year-old woman living on her own, who needs her son every time she has a maintenance problem in the apartment, and her daughter to sort out her bank statements. Her health is fine, thank God, but though her mind is still sharp, she's become increasingly forgetful. She continues to teach Hebrew to Sudanese immigrants twice a week, but twice in the last month she's misplaced her phone and had to have Shlomi backtrack through her day with her until luckily they located it both times, once at the counter of the Super Pharm, and once at Gordon Pool, where she swims twice a week and the lifeguards know her. After that, Tamar started to notice other lapses, too. She called her friend Katie, a neuroscientist, who told her not to worry, there was no reason to believe it was the onset of Alzheimer's, it was just that the messenger in her frontal cortex that got sent to the hippocampus was growing a little slower, a little more tired. It wasn't that the memory was eroded, it was all still very much there, but as the brain ages, the messenger sent to retrieve the memory gets weak and lazy, and sometimes lost along the way.

In other words, her mother is getting old. It's nothing Tamar hasn't already grasped. When her father was suddenly felled in the supermarket by a crushing pain in the chest, and died less than an hour later at the hospital before Tamar or Shlomi could get there, she'd understood something all at once about the fragility of her parents' lives, understood that they had entered the stage in which death would now be always around the corner. Her mother isn't a fool, and she isn't frail either, but she is aging, and everyone knows how easy it is to prey on the elderly. Isn't it their responsibility, Shlomi's and hers, to make sure that their mother isn't taken advantage of? A strange man, two strange men in fact, show up at her door without any warning and claim that a Husband has been found that their mother has never lost! Claim that someone who never belonged to her in fact belongs to her in the most intimate way, with all of the responsibilities, emotional not to mention financial, that that implies. Has Israel become so broken and corrupt, Tamar wonders, so wildly chutzpadik, that having failed to put aside the resources to take care of the very people it was founded to provide refuge for— the lost and dispossessed—having instead drowned all of its resources in defense, and the prime minister's taste for cigars, pink champagne, and jewelry, that some crackpot in the administration, the Head Clown of Public Health, has hatched the crooked plot to deliver these poor old uncared-for people to innocent people's doors, asserting that they belong to them, and so are their responsibility?

Is there no end, she thinks, flopping again from her back to her stomach while Remy breathes heavily at her side, is there really no *end* to the uses and abuses of the Holocaust they will come up with? Here they are, riffing off a deep emotional chord in the country's history, playing on the moving stories her mother's generation grew up with, which happened far too infrequently but were so often told, of fathers and husbands, wives and sisters, lost during the war and presumed dead, only to be miraculously dredged up by the Red Cross and reunited with their loved ones. Rescued from the lost and the dead in some hellish DP camp, packed onto a boat to Haifa, and in a moving ceremony of the impossible becoming possible, the unreal becoming real, which after all was to be the hallmark, the specialty, of that about-to-be-born country, delivered into the arms of the one who lost them, who presumably never took them for granted again. And now here was Social Services, or Special Services, or whatever they called themselves, claiming even now, seventy years on, to be turning up, in the form of little old men in shapeless hats, all the love that was lost? And, so that no opportunity for hypocrisy should be missed, at the very same moment when they were sending their agents out with a plan to thrust these unclaimed old Jews into other people's homes and hands, they were sending out the police to round up the Sudanese in Florentine for deportation, and to pluck out of their homes Filipino children who had been born in Israel, whose first language was Hebrew and grew up singing "Ha'Tikva," to throw them into jail before kicking them out of the country they'd grown up in for good. What kind of fools did they think they were dealing with?

She leaps out of bed and pulls on her robe, the puffy chenille one the kids got for her birthday a few years back, as comfortable as it is unflattering, yanks her phone from the plug, and marches into the kitchen. If Shlomi isn't prepared to do anything about this, if he is happy to just sit by and let their mother be conned by this character and the agency acting in support of his audacity, then she will have to see to it on her own.

She calls her mother. It's already eight thirty in the morning in Israel, and either she will be getting ready to go to the pool or preparing for her class. And yet when her mother answers after four or five rings, there is the sound of roaring and children shouting, and, after a moment, a booming voice warning someone of the rip current on the other side of the ropes.

Hold on, I can't hear you! her mother shouts.

Where are you? Tamar asks, because it sounds like the beach, and her mother hates the beach, is always complaining that the sea is filthy, and accusing the packed cafés on the beach of highway robbery. On one of the few occasions that Tamar can remember her mother agreeing to take her and Shlomi to the beach when they were little, Shlomi got stung by a jellyfish, which only cemented their mother's poor opinion of the place. She is content to look at the sea from the comfort of the promenade, which she walks on her way to and from the pool twice or three times a week, but otherwise she is one of the few residents of the city who has more or less turned her back on it.

I can't hear you, her mother repeats, I'm at the beach.

What are you doing there?

We're having a coffee.

As in, you and him?

Who?

The Husband.

Her mother says nothing.

I spoke to Shlomi, Mom. Here I was laughing on the phone at your story, but you sure took your time getting to the punch line of the joke.

What joke?

That he stayed! That you accepted a little old man that someone claimed is your lost husband into your apartment, into—and here Tamar pauses, because for the first time it occurs to her that her mother might have gone even further than inviting him to sit in the chair by the window, that she might have accepted him into her bed.

Her mother laughs.

What's so funny? Tamar demands.

He isn't so little, her mother says, and then she hears her say to him, It's only Tamar, my daughter, Tamar.

We need to talk, Mom. I don't understand why you're going along with this, and I'm concerned.

About what? I'm having a coffee on the beach, that's all. I'll call you later. And why are you up in the middle of the night, anyway? Iris stayed out late again? You're finally getting paid back for all of the nights you stayed out when you were her age. But it's good for her, let her enjoy. Look how serious you turned out to be.

On this new, lighter note her mother hangs up, the roaring of the waves is cut off, and Tamar is returned to the silence of her kitchen in the suburban street where she has lived for the last twelve years, since Iris was three.

Not so little! she repeats. But all that comes back is the hum of the Subzero, a sound one only ever hears when alone.

IN THE DAYS that follow, Tamar gathers from Shlomi that though the Husband has not yet moved in with their mother, he is spending a lot of time with her. He is from Hungary, his Hebrew is not, it turns out, as eloquent as Alterman's, he only knows a poem or two of Alterman's by heart, which he recites at moments when his Hebrew fails him. Their mother, however, is used to the broken Hebrew of immigrants, and is an excellent teacher, too; already the Husband is wearing her corrections well. Why he was lost for so long, why he only came to be found at this late stage, remains unclear: neither Shlomi nor her mother can explain any of it to her with clarity. He was extracted from Hungary some years ago—two, or three, or maybe five—or he had extracted himself, and since then had been living in Netanya, where he'd passed his time playing cards at the Hungarian club until someone had recognized him to be, or he had revealed himself to be, the lost Husband.

It doesn't seem to matter to either Shlomi or her mother that the math doesn't add up: that he was only a child during the war, and so couldn't have been married back then to anyone, not to mention that her mother has no connection with Hungary, has never even stepped foot in Hungary. While the Husband was stuck behind the Iron Curtain, her mother grew from a girl into a woman in Jerusalem, attended Hebrew University, and met her father, got married, moved to Tel Aviv, and became pregnant with Tamar, and four years later with Shlomi. Why, Tamar asks, when that curtain finally lifted and let in the brief light of democracy, had the Husband not made any gestures that would have allowed him to be found? Why was it that only in recent years, as the Hungarian government moved toward the far right and became more and more overt in its state-sponsored xenophobia and its glorification of Nazi collaborators, and the brief light of democracy dimmed toward autocracy, did it finally dawn on the Husband, who had no family around him, whose neighbors in the small town where he lived were also getting more brazen in their anti-Semitism, to put up his hand, to raise the white flag of the lost who wish to be found? Is there not a statute of limitations on being able to claim that one is lost? And what in the world does her mother have to do with any of this?

For a brief while Tamar even entertains the idea that her mother has a secret story she's kept from the rest of the family. Her mother has always been there for them, has always given Tamar, Shlomi, and their father enough of herself for them to feel gifted with her attention. When Iris was born and demanded everything, Tamar wondered how her mother managed it, this trick of making them feel seen and heard, watched and loved, while at the same time she kept something away, a small portion of herself reserved for elsewhere. Tamar herself doesn't know how to do it. Either she gives too much or not enough, either she feels overwhelmed or selfish. She waited to have Iris until after she'd finished her research and set up her practice. David had wanted children from the very beginning, but she insisted on giving herself time. But when she finally agreed to get pregnant and Iris arrived, the baby was colicky and never stopped crying. It took every ounce of energy Tamar had to soothe her, so that from the very beginning her only choice as a mother, or so it had seemed, had been to devote herself entirely: to race around the kitchen island to keep the baby wildly bouncing in the carrier, to hum and shush and swing and sway and rock and let Iris suck all of the blood out of her pinkie, out of her life, to give up on seeing friends because if she didn't possess all of her mother's attention, Iris was inconsolable. And even after the nearly twelve months of colic ended, the child remained sensitive to everything; to little Iris, the world, however wondrous, was at base a menacing place, and Tamar was needed at all times to mitigate this danger. Was it something she'd done? Had she somehow communicated this grim and anxious outlook? More than likely. And yet she herself hadn't been that sort of child. Her mother had always said she was an easy baby, though now Tamar thought that probably said more about her mother than about her. Raising Iris was a project that for a long time exhausted and drained her, which is why it took nearly five years for her to come around to having Remy. And even then, she thought she was only doing it for Iris's sake, so that her daughter wouldn't be alone. During that difficult period— catching sight of herself in the mirror and trying to work out where she'd gone, and if any of her would ever come back again, if whatever made her essentially herself had been lost forever, bartered for a baby—she would find herself wondering what her mother's secret was. What her mother knew or possessed that allowed her to give just enough of herself, without ever giving herself fully away. Only now does it occur to Tamar that maybe her mother had something of her own, something, or someone, she'd needed and so taken for herself, which made all of that giving possible. And yet even if she'd had a secret life, even if she'd found her own way to receive back, through unknown channels, some of the love she gave, it couldn't have been with him, the lost Husband, any more than it could have been with a man from Nairobi or Shanghai. The facts just didn't line up.

So what if it's absurd? Shlomi finally admits on the phone, two nights after their mother and the Husband take a picnic to the beach near Herzliya. What's the big deal if it isn't hurting anyone? There's nothing to be worried about, he asserts, holding to his unique-in-the-family position. The Husband is harmless, he has no designs on their mother's money or her apartment. He's a charming man, their mother is enjoying herself. She's been alone since their father died. Why should they deny her some company and a bit of fun by being sticklers for the facts?

Tamar is about to assert that she, too, has been alone since her divorce, and he doesn't see her taking in random men, does he? If she could reduce all of the words her patients spill in her office to a single, plaintive truth, it is that in the end everyone is alone, and the sooner one comes to terms with it, celebrates it, even, the sooner one can begin to live beyond the long shadow of anguish and anxiety. A woman living on her own is not a condition that required the emergency airlift of a man, she wants to argue, on the contrary—

But as the words are about to leave her mouth, she realizes that her brother might be right. Maybe she *is* being defensive. Her mother, who has always been there to answer her calls, is now otherwise engaged, and maybe it's gotten to her a bit. They've shared a condition, haven't they? Two independent women without husbands, managing just fine on their own, thank you very much. In its way, it's only strengthened the bond between them. Neither of them suffered overly without a husband. Their situations were different, of course: her parents stayed together for forty-seven years before death put an end to it, whereas Tamar and David chose to break their marriage after only ten. Tamar can claim the position of being not interested in another husband, of being "beyond husbandry," as she sometimes puts it to her friends, whereas for her mother the subject of another husband is—was, until then—a moot point. But even if her mother chose to keep her husband and Tamar did not, something in them has always seemed to her in tacit agreement about the relative peace and quiet of being without one, its lack of demand after a long period of trying to fulfill a high level of demand. She likes that her mother never goes on, the way the mothers of other divorced women she knows go on, about how she should find someone while she still has her looks. And if Tamar does eventually stumble on a man she wishes to be bound to—in other words, a man other than the thirty-two-year-old electronic musician she slept with until she got tired of doing his laundry or he left for Peru, or the trial lawyer who had an out-size personality but, in the end, a shrunken heart—her mother will no doubt be happy for her. Is she happy for her mother?

She calls Katie.

Maybe I feel abandoned? Tamar suggests, as the Metro North train pulls out of University Heights on its way to the city.

Or just a little jealous, Katie says.

Jealous? Of a little old Hungarian? He makes mulberry jam. And they play chess together.

Of your mother finding love again, Katie says.

Tamar sits holding the phone to her ear, watching the chain-link fences and telephone poles fly by as the train hurtles toward Harlem. Love. It has not yet dawned on her that it might be that. Because what are the odds, really? That somewhere in the annals of Special Services, that little-known agency of the state, there is some Israeli Cupid at work, busily matching widows and widowers with a greater success rate than Tinder?

Uh-uh, she says, there's no way. She just met him! It'll probably be over in a week. Trust me, she assures her, even though Katie doesn't have a horse in the race.

But the following Saturday, Tamar comes into the kitchen fresh from the shower and finds Remy, who always FaceTimes with her mother on Saturday mornings, learning a card trick from the Husband. She hears his voice first, a deep tenor with an accent refined and educated, savvy and world-weary, soaked in a broth of middle European languages, an old-world accent that went out of production after 1945. She steps closer, careful to stay out of the camera's range. She can see his face on the screen, and in the top left corner Remy's eyes, beaming behind the hand of cards he is clutching. Until then the Husband has not been entirely real. He's been only an old man in a hat, utterly absurd in his way. But now here he is, talking to her son. Charming him, just as he charmed her mother and Shlomi. She steps into view, casting a shadow over Remy's bright face.

I'm Tamar, she says coolly. The daughter.

The Husband says nothing, but his heavy-lidded eyes, full of intelligence, take her in. He doesn't look at all the way she imagined, at once wiser and somewhat younger, more alive, with blue eyes and a white beard she hadn't expected that is neatly trimmed to make visible his full lips, lips that would not have been out of place on a child. They regard each other with raised hackles, and yet only one of them, Tamar thinks with satisfaction, is a scavenger.

So what are your plans? she demands, while Remy watches both of their faces on the screen.

Plans for what? the Husband asks, surprised. Behind him she can see the windows of her mother's living room, and, on the wall just to the right of his head, a framed photograph of her and Shlomi at Iris and Remy's ages, her with a whale-spout ponytail in a scrunchie, and Shlomi channeling the Karate Kid.

Your gig in Netanya is up, or what? You can still stay there, or you're planning to move to Tel Aviv?

She'd intended to say "planning to move into our mother's apartment," but something about his gaze, deerlike, makes her swerve at the last instant.

Netanya is finished, he says simply, without further explanation.

Remy, unable to parse the dialogue, glances up at his mother.

We were in the middle of a trick, he pleads.

So you were, Tamar says, raising an eyebrow at the Husband so that her point will not be lost. So you were. And, turning on her heel, she stomps off to brew the coffee.

4

——

March, which came in like a lion and went out like a lamb, deposited in its path the lost Husband, and in mid-May Shlomi's baby is born in Nepal because surrogacy for gay men remains illegal in Israel. Two weeks later, he and Dan fly with the infant back to Tel Aviv, and in the third week of June, the day after Iris and Remy finish school, Tamar packs their suitcases as usual and goes over the plant-watering schedule with the house sitter, a Columbia grad student who was a woman last year, but now is a man. Tamar and the kids have spent July in Tel Aviv every year since she and David divorced, and she often stays on in August while the kids fly to meet him wherever he's decided to spend his vacation. The Columbia student, who was Jessica for the last three summers, is now Kevin, and because Tamar was not present for the transformation, she has the impression, however wrongheaded and absurd, that it happened simply, without a great deal of fuss, just like everything Jessica has ever done. For the last three summers they kept everything in perfect order; more than perfect, really, because when Tamar returned in late August, it was always to a house more organized and well run than the one she'd left, the minor repairs that had accumulated over the year having been seen to, all the burned-out light bulbs replaced, and while this at first delighted her, in the wake of the delight there was left a feeling that she was slightly superfluous, that she was not really needed by her life in New York, just as she was not really needed by her life, what was left of it, in Tel Aviv. One could argue whether or not this is true— there are her patients, her children, her mother, her friends, in short, many people who need her—but regardless of its validity, it is the thought of someone whose roots are sown in two places and so can never grow deeply enough in either. Always on the plane back to Israel Tamar feels the excitement of finally going home, only to land and remember why she left.

For Iris and Remy it's less complicated. They love to visit their grandmother, love the beach, which Tamar takes them to in the evenings, love the food, the late bedtimes, the access to a warm, relaxed updraft of freedom so different from the climate in New York. And they are over the moon about meeting the baby. They've already FaceTimed with their newborn cousin, and Remy has insisted on packing his little rollaway with toys and books he's grown out of, to pass on to the five-week-old, who does not yet have a name because Shlomi and Dan are still "getting to know him." The kids cannot wait to hold the baby, they say as they are patted down at the special gate for the United flight from Newark to Israel. Iris, who is fifteen, which in communities the world over and through time makes her of acceptable childbearing age, is going to "eat the baby up," and Remy is going to see if he can be the first to make him smile. Tucked into the pocket of Remy's rollaway is also the pack of cards that has gone everywhere with him the last weeks, at the ready for the practice or performance of a sleight of hand. But neither Remy nor Iris mention anything about meeting the Husband, having gathered, through looks or tones or curt phrases, a measure of their mother's opinion. A few days earlier, Tamar overheard Remy in Iris's room, telling her that the Husband had collaborated with Erdős, and so had an Erdős number of one. If he had collaborated with someone who had collaborated with Erdős, he would have an Erdős number of two, and if he had collaborated with someone who had collaborated with someone who had collaborated with Erdős, it would be a three. Someone who had never collaborated with Erdős would have an Erdős number of infinity. But he had a one! And he was going to take Remy to see a Maccabi game.

Who's Erdős? asked Iris.

A genius who wrote more mathematical papers than anyone, solved some of the hardest problems in the world, and lived out of his suitcase, Remy informed her with a note of pride.

But the Husband is no longer living out of a suitcase. He has bettered Erdős on that problem, Tamar thinks, having read up on Erdős in Wikipedia. He has refuted Erdős's theory that women capture men and enslave them into marriage, and has offered himself as a lost husband, and so has won a place for his suitcase in the basement storage unit, having gone and unpacked all of its contents and laid them in what were formerly her father's drawers.

Tamar waited, in the week before their departure, for her mother to say something about the living arrangements. They always stayed with her when they visited, Tamar sleeping in her old bedroom, and Iris and Remy sharing Shlomi's, all of them taking turns for the bathroom with the shower that has next to no pressure. How did her mother imagine it would work if the Husband was there, too? The apartment, which always just managed four people, would be strained by five, especially if one was a stranger. Perhaps her mother was waiting for her to volunteer to stay at Shlomi and Dan's place in Jaffa, big enough for the sprawling, extended Arab family it was once built for. But Tamar didn't offer, and her mother didn't ask, and so now they are headed in a taxi for Tchernichovsky Street.

Ilana is waiting outside, and as the kids fly into her arms, Tamar has a chance to take in the subtle changes in her mother's appearance—her hair that is a few shades lighter, the copper dusted with gold, her leopard-print leggings, even further out on the limb on which her mother's fashion taste has always rested, and on her hip a quilted leather fanny pack with a fake Chanel logo. Feeling around inside it for her keys, her mother gaily informs them that she hasn't lost a thing since she started using it, she keeps it on from the moment she gets up until the moment she goes to sleep, and it has solved the problem of misplacing things: everything that comes out of it goes right back in. As she says it, affectionately patting the plump pouch like a baby's bottom, Tamar guesses from the delight in her mother's voice that it was the Husband's idea, that her mother's pleasure in the solution is also her pleasure in his ingenuity, and the fact that he's devoted his special intelligence to her little problem. Climbing the steps behind the swaying fanny pack with the gilded double C, while Remy rides up in the tiny elevator with the luggage, Tamar steels herself for the encounter that is about to take place. But when her mother unlocks the door and the kids tumble in with the suitcases, there is no one else there. Tamar inhales the familiar smell of home and childhood. And only after the first, strong notes of her mother's cooking, the old building, and Israeli laundry detergent fade away does she discover underneath it all the musky odor of men's cologne.

Where is he? she asks, still sniffing.

Who? her mother asks, but with a telltale twitch of her eyelid, as if the wizened Husband who once collaborated with Erdős had grabbed his hat and shimmied out through the window just as they came in through the door, Erdős who chose for his gravestone the epitaph "Finally I am growing stupider no more."

Grandma! shouts Remy, racing into the kitchen with the pack of cards just in time to get her mother off the hook. Can I show you a trick?

But even if the Husband came out of nowhere and nothing, it does not mean her mother can send him back to nowhere and nothing whenever it's convenient: in the bathroom, Tamar discovers a toothbrush with flattened bristles in the glass next to her mother's.

THAT EVENING THEY all take a taxi to Jaffa to visit the new baby. He has a head of black hair, but otherwise he is the spitting image of Tamar and Shlomi's father. From deep within the turquoise wrap that Dan already ties like an expert, the infant looks out in great peace, as if he has already seen the world beyond and has come back to observe, with bottomless compassion, the fucked-up earthly things they've all gotten up to. When at last he is unpacked from the carrier and handed round, and Tamar lays him down on her thighs, he bestows on her his cloudy, beatific gaze. On and on everyone goes about how he looks exactly like Eli—Eli down to the little cleft in his chin! but an Eli without a bark, an Eli without claws!— and Tamar can't help but feel the real point being made by her mother and brother, the not-so-subtle subtext, is that her father is looking down on it all—Shlomi's marriage, her divorce, the arrival of the Husband who plans to replace him—with a vast and yielding acceptance, with the kind of tolerance that had not been available to him on this side of life. It was not an accident that Shlomi waited until their father died before marrying Dan. Nor that Tamar hung on in her marriage as long as she did, until, less than a year after her father was gone, she finally let go. Eli's strong opinions, and the volume and intensity with which he expressed them, made it easier to just work around him rather than confront his forcefulness head-on. They'd learned it early on from their mother, who would let their father bluster and blow, and afterward, once he was asleep, or at work, or with his back turned, would let them have what they'd asked for, or find a quiet way to show them how to take it for themselves.

The baby lurches and grabs Tamar's finger. It really *is* eerie, she thinks, the way this nameless child brought into existence from a combination of Shlomi's sperm, the egg of Dan's sister, the womb and sweat of a Nepali woman, and a dash of fairy dust, looks the spitting image of their father. How did it work?

But, all the same, she isn't having it. Her cantankerous father has not regrouped in Nepal to send back to them a beneficent message. Eli would have had plenty to say about it all, and it wouldn't have been pretty. Eli, the doyen of Israeli shlumpadik, who wore baggy cargo pants and the same shirts until the buttons fell off, who had no feel for the elegance of math, would have crushed the Husband's brown hat in one hand and told him what he could do with his jam and his Erdős.

Prying her finger loose from the baby's grip, she passes him off to Iris, who takes him onto her chest as if she knows exactly what to do with babies, having been one herself. Tamar goes over to the plate-glass window and looks out at the sea. Had she stayed in Israel, she might have woken each day to a view like this, one that went all the way out to the horizon. But instead she went to New York to do her PhD, married David, and somewhere along the way lost her sense of expansiveness. It wasn't David's fault any more than it was her own. She had simply arrived too late to the conversation that might have made clear to her the many unconsidered possibilities. To listen to her patients in their twenties and thirties, monogamy was a great beached whale, its bloated, rotten carcass stinking to high hell, and the sooner one got away from it, the better. Whether the wave of polyamory they were all trying to ride would ever really carry anyone, or whether jealousy and the horror of instability would always sink them, Tamar couldn't say. Look at Shlomi: he has ridden the high crest of free love, has loved and been loved by all of Mykonos and Ibiza, but in the end he wanted what everyone has wanted for as long as people have been remembering themselves—how did the poem go? *Not universal love, but to be loved alone.*

She turns away from the window in time to see Iris hold her cousin in the air to sniff his bottom. She has always tried to instill in Iris the conviction that she doesn't need to get married, doesn't need the stability of the conjugal life to ground her. But to look at her daughter now, her nose in the baby's bum, it seems more likely that Iris, *davka*, will be married by twenty-five, and remain so until she is surrounded by grandchildren at her dying husband's bedside, rubbing his cold feet. Tamar turns back to the window and watches the blue waves roll in from far away. What is the good of expansiveness if one doesn't expand? What is the good of so much possibility if one only feels it as a widening in the chest while driving down a country road at dusk, or when, standing still in the rooms of the house when the children are shared out at their father's, one suddenly becomes aware of a silence so pure that it raises the hairs on the back of one's neck?

I've got it! Iris shouts. Everyone turns to her. How about Rafael? He's a perfect Rafael! she exclaims, holding up the baby so that all can look at him in this new light. Her uncles exchange a thoughtful look. Shlomi still likes Micah, but Dan wants to stay away from the Bible and its implications. He stands looking at the baby with his hands on his hips, the empty carrier slung across his shoulder where twenty years ago there hung a machine gun.

What about Tom? he asks. Sandor came up with it the other day, and I have to say that it's stuck.

It's the first time Tamar has heard anyone utter the Husband's name. The first time, in fact, that anyone has mentioned him since she arrived in Israel. She's half begun to wonder, despite the toothbrush and the smell of cologne, whether as part of some elaborate ploy they've made him up altogether.

Doesn't he look like a Tom? Dan asks.

He looks like an Eli, is what he looks like, her mother insists.

I like Tom, Remy offers.

Iris turns the baby back to herself, to study his features once more.

Actually, me too, she agrees.

Shlomi gives a look that suggests he doesn't disagree, and all eyes turn expectantly to Tamar. But what she's really being asked, what it is that she would be agreeing to, she can't exactly say. And so she sighs and turns back to the sea, as if there was something out there, something coming from far off, that requires her presence to receive it.

5

The following day the baby comes down with something. They all used the antibacterial gel that Dan squirted into their palms, but nevertheless the baby has woken with a stuffy nose, and soon he is running a fever. Shlomi, who is against worrying, insists it is only a cold. But the fever climbs, and when the hitherto peaceful baby starts to scream and has trouble breathing while he feeds, Dan calls a doctor. It is three in the morning by then, but his old friend Yuli, a pediatrician, drives over in her car. When she sees the baby's labored breathing and listens to the congestion in his chest, she tells them he has a bronchial infection and insists on driving them to the hospital. There the baby is given a chest X-ray, admitted to the pediatric ICU, placed in a metal crib under an oxygen tent, hooked to an IV and cardiac monitor, and fitted with a tiny clamp on his finger that sends rays of light through it, so that the doctors can keep track of the oxygen level in his blood. He has a respiratory virus that, while common enough in adults, can take a five-week-old's life. By the time Tamar, Ilana, and the kids get to the Children's Center at Ichilov, Shlomi is frightened. He stares at the baby's vital signs rising and falling on the monitor, or slouches next to the crib, stroking his child with a hand slipped under the plastic tent. A nurse comes and sticks a long tube far down the baby's throat to suction out the mucus, while Shlomi looks on in horror, crossing and recrossing his arms over his chest. It is a procedure that will have to be done every few hours in the days that follow. The baby doesn't have enough energy left to scream, but tears run down from the corners of his gray eyes. Remy starts to sob, and Tamar takes him downstairs with the excuse of buying her brother and Dan a coffee.

Is Tom going to be okay? Remy asks, pushing his forehead into her stomach.

Yes, she says, though she has no authority to declare as much. Tom will be just fine.

But from then on, the baby has a name. A name that pins him to life, that stands in opposition to the nothing and nowhere that hovers like a shadow just outside the hospital room door. A name both of his fathers can cry out on the second day, when the Code Red sounds and the emergency team comes flying into the room, ready to intubate the baby, a procedure that will no longer leave him to breathe on his own. A name that the Code Red team, gathered around the crib, can refer to in his chart once the numbers on the monitor begin slowly to drift up again, and for the time being the emergency has passed, and his fragile life holds.

IT IS NOT until the third day that the Husband appears at the hospital. He arrives carrying a plastic Castro bag from which he removes homemade sandwiches packed in tinfoil for everyone, and a large thermos of sweet tea. The brown felt hat has been replaced with a straw one for summer, which he hangs on a hook behind the door. He has been away, and came as fast as he could, he explains. He does not say where. Maybe the others know, or maybe for them it is irrelevant: the point is that he is here with them now. Remy and Iris greet him with smiles, glancing at their mother, whom they seem to hope will not say or do anything untoward. Tamar watches him take her own mother's hand. He doesn't assert himself into the family dynamic, and yet at the same time he seems simply to be accepted there, with kindness and gratitude. Watching him, Tamar thinks of something Katie sometimes said: that there is no man anywhere so difficult, that there is not some woman somewhere dying to take care of him. If, having had enough of being a woman, she decides to throw in the towel at last—if such a thing were actually possible without extreme hardship, and every form of pain—could Tamar also give herself over to those that would bring her up the stairs to an unknown door, where a woman would be waiting, perhaps a whole family, to take her in with open arms and no questions asked?

Ilana insists that they all take a break and go out to sit under the trees in the playground for a while. Shlomi and Dan haven't left the hospital since they arrived, and the sun and air will do them good. Tamar goes down with everyone, but once outside realizes that she's forgotten her handbag with her sunglasses. Returning upstairs, she pauses at the door of Tom's room and looks in to find the Husband sitting next to his crib in a shaft of light from the window, talking quietly to the baby in his strange language. The moment has no logic, it exists outside of reason, nor does it carry anything inauthentic. No one and nothing has any more right to it than the new child, foreign like every baby who arrives from the unknown, and the foreign old man who now begins to softly sing to him.

On the fifth day, Tom finally turns the corner. He is in the clear, and that evening the oxygen tent is removed, and when Remy puts down the card trick he has been practicing and goes over to look into the open crib, Tom looks up at him and beams. On the morning of the sixth they promise that after a final chest X-ray, Tom will be able to go home, but they keep him one last night, so that it is not until the morning of the seventh day that he is finally released, returned to the family the same way he came to them, only now with the awareness that the people who arrive to us from nowhere and nothing are only ever that: a gift, received without our having known to ask, with only the wonder of how life delivers and delivers.

To Be a Man

My Father

My boys are standing at the edge of the jetty, and either they will jump or they won't jump. It is early summer, June, under the great bell of the sky, on the island on which I was raised. The waves are coming in from such a long way off that no one can say when or where their turbulence began, only that they are the transmittance of an energy that finally breaks here, and resolves into the shore. I watch them, my two boys, from the sand. My father, unusually quiet today, wearing a hat against the sun, watches too. He isn't yet old, but at this very moment I can't recall exactly how old he is. If his life seems long to me, it's because he has changed more than anyone I know. One day, over the course of many years—there is no other way to put it—he took all his great anger out to sea, let the wind out of its sails, and came back home without it. Came back home with a stillness and patience where once the rocking fury had been.

Sometimes I forget my own age too. When people ask the ages of my boys, I round upward to give myself time to get used to where they are going. But while my father doesn't have so very much time left, and I have some, my boys still have all the time in the world. The younger one does a little dance on the edge of the jetty. The older one tilts back his head, spreads his arms, and shouts something toward the sky.

I watch my boys and talk, and my father listens. Life, I say, or am trying to say, which is always happening on so many levels, all at the same time.

Broken Ribs

I

That summer, while her boys are on vacation with their father, she goes to visit her lover in Berlin.

"You see," he says, leaning down toward her and lowering his voice so that those passing by won't hear, "one thing you don't know about me is that I like to serve."

It is a surprising thing to hear, coming from a man two meters tall and built like a heavyweight. In fact, he is an amateur boxer; or rather was one for many years, until a month ago, when an attack of *Schwindel*—of vertigo—briefly hospitalized him, turned up a scar in his brain, and put an end to it. And yet, though he claims that he will never step foot in the ring again, and is employed as an editor at a highly respected newspaper, she still privately refers to him, both to her friends and herself, as the German Boxer. It is easier than using his name, which means "little gift from the gods"—because of that, and because calling him the German Boxer highlights their differences, and preserves a sense of ironic distance that keeps her grounded in the new land she's recently discovered, like some Christopher Columbus of the soul: the land of being unattached and free.

They are walking around Schlachtensee—a long, thin lake at the edge of the Grunewald Forest—discussing whether or not eighty years ago he would have been a Nazi. The German Boxer thinks it is moral grandstanding to claim that he would not have been, as most everyone else in his generation claims, but now he goes beyond the usual argument of how he would have been shaped by historical forces that would have made his participation nearly inevitable, to offer the particular vulnerabilities of his own character.

"I am *exactly* the kind of person they would have recruited for the Napola," he says, referring to the elite preparatory schools where they groomed the strong, obedient, and relatively clever German youth into leaders of the SS. "I've always overly idolized my mentors, and strove to fulfill every last demand they made of me, because it struck fear in me to imagine failing their expectations. That, along with my size and build, makes me just the sort of person they would have wanted. And, being wanted, I would have felt honored. It's my weakness for honor and praise, you see, that would have sent me right into the ranks of the SS."

"Plus you would have loved the uniform," she adds, thinking

of the row of white shirts tailored in London that hang on a bar in the sunlight of his bedroom, of his suits made in Naples not only to his measurements but also to his precise taste (no silk, no lining at all, only materials rough to the touch), his winter coat of wool so finely stitched that he avoids putting his hands in the pockets for fear of ruining it. Of his white leather boxing gloves, handmade by Winning in Japan to fit his slim fingers and wrists. She does not offer this evidence gladly. She would prefer to believe that the man she is sleeping with could not have been, under any circumstances, a Nazi. But by now she knows him well enough that she can't truly disagree.

Along the shore of the lake, lovers spoon in the sunlight or under the alders, kissing or lazily stroking each other's half-naked bodies, and whenever they pass an attractive couple, the German Boxer points them out with a sign of appreciation, or maybe even envy. He was happily married for nearly a decade, blazingly happy, as he describes it, until his wife, an actress, left him for the man who played Lancelot to her Guinevere in the Volksbühne. Since then he's lost the feeling he's had all his life of being blessed and untouchable. Those close to him see this as a positive development, he admits, since until his divorce felled him, he was often insufferable. But he has been broken by it, and he would have preferred to remain happy and insufferable than whatever he is now.

Arriving at the beer garden at the eastern end of the lake, they stop to have a drink. It is a Sunday, and the tables covered with red-and-white-checked cloths are crowded with Germans enjoying their nature. Joyful shouts of children float up from the water's edge. The German Boxer is telling her that her older son's lankiness and long arms, which he's seen in a photo, would make him an excellent boxer, and it does not seem necessary to her to repeat that her son would never box, that her son is nearly as far from boxing as he is from being German. Not finding a foothold, the conversation moves on to Oktoberfest, and he begins to explain to her what a dirndl is.

"But you would have *killed*?" she asks now, though perhaps with less incredulity than she might have expressed toward someone who had not, on occasion, knocked out a stranger with a single punch, or nearly snapped the wooden bars of her headboard because in the midst of orgasm he experienced an uncontainable desire to destroy something.

"Of course I would have killed," he says. "Killed while believing—having been built to believe—that I was doing the right thing."

"I could never kill anyone," she insists.

Over the top of his beer glass, the German Boxer eyes her with a look of polite skepticism. And it is true that no sooner has she made this assertion than her mind begins involuntarily to supply exceptions.

When, a few days later, she makes reference in a text to him showing up at her door in 1941 in leather boots, he replies that one thing he could *not* have done was kill innocent people. This seems in contradiction to what he so plainly asserted while walking in placid sunshine around the lake, but when she writes back to clarify which people it was that he had been so certain he could kill, her text remains unanswered, hanging in WhatsApp limbo, stamped with only a single gray check, because the German Boxer likes to turn his phone off when he feels finished with it. Later, when she meets him for dinner at a vegetarian restaurant in Mitte, he says that of course he couldn't have knocked on people's doors and deported or executed them. What kind of person does she think he is? When he said he could kill people, he meant *in battle*, since he was sure that he would have been assigned to the Waffen SS and sent to the front. She does not have the wherewithal just then to ask what makes him so sure he wouldn't have been assigned to the Gestapo, or the Allgemeine SS responsible for enforcing the Nazi racial policies, or even the Death's Head units that oversaw the concentration and extermination camps.

They sit in silence, waiting for their dumplings to come. After a few moments, the German Boxer suggests that he might be wrong. After all, he says, his grandfather was in constant trouble with the Nazis because he'd allowed Gypsies to stay on his land, his great-grandfather was murdered in Aktion T4, and his father was the sort of man who refused to follow anyone. No, perhaps he wouldn't have been a Nazi after all—let's hope as much, he says. She nods. In truth, she agrees, their conversation is an impossible one, given that whoever he was now would not have been who he'd have been back then, shaped as he would have been by different forces, and whoever he'd have been then did not exist.

Though naturally she continues to think about it.

2
———

A mutual friend set them up in New York, and over email they agreed to have dinner the following night. He asked if they could meet on the later side, since he would be boxing in the afternoon. Where did he box? she asked; she was curious to see this. In fact, she had never seen anyone box, not even on TV, since brutality and blood made her queasy. He wrote that she wouldn't want to meet him after he sparred, that it was the kind of gym where no one showered, but that if he liked her after tomorrow, he would take her to the gym and they would fight; until then it would remain a secret gym. "Nobody knows me there, or what I do or what I think or what I want," he wrote. She read his email three times, then replied that he ought to be careful, that she was deadly. She didn't know exactly why she wrote that. Maybe because of the arrogance in his phrasing, the indirect challenge of it: *If I still like you.* Because of the sense of pride it tripped loose in her, even if she knew he was writing in a language not his own, without the nuance he had in German, and because she wanted him to know that she was someone who had—who had always had—a certain power over men. Or because she wished to imply that whatever was explosive in him was also explosive in her, that there might be a parity there, and maybe more than a parity: that the scales of explosiveness, of a form of strength, might even tip in her favor. Which may or may not have been grandstanding.

"My ribs have a tendency to break," he wrote back. "Please be careful when destroying me." In other words, he knew exactly what to do with her. Caught her and spun her around and drew her close; knew how to work her, knew just what a mix of strength and vulnerability in a man can do to certain women, of which she was apparently one. As it was, after this brief exchange she knew that she would take him home to bed.

When she arrived at the restaurant, he was already there, the way German trains are always already there, waiting in the station. His size was something else again. It was impossible not to notice him, looming a head or even two above everyone around him. If someone asked her in that moment—the waiter, for example, going past with his tray held high—whether she liked being made to feel physically small next to a man, she would have had to answer yes. Yes, but with an asterisk! *Physically small but spiritually powerful. In other words, she liked him to be a wolf in sheep's clothing until she said he could be a wolf, and then he should be pure wolf with no trace of the sheep for the duration of time they would spend fucking in her bed, after which he should go back to being someone who wouldn't in a million years think of grabbing her throat when he wanted something. Was this a problem? And one more thing: from time to time he should be very slow and gentle when he went about blowing her house down.

He handed her a stem of tiny, pale purple flowers. She thought he'd picked them on the way, but later it turned out that he'd bought a whole bouquet, but gave the rest away to a pregnant woman on the subway who'd admired them and asked who they were for, because at that moment it occurred to him that he'd bought a bouquet of flowers for a stranger, which might have been overdoing it. They were shown to their table. The restaurant was dim and warm, the walls lined with the old glass cabinets of the pharmacy the place had been until, after having been boarded up for decades, it reopened as an Italian restaurant. Whenever a waiter or waitress came to the table, the German Boxer stopped what he was saying to smile and thank them for whatever they had just set down.

The conversation moved lightly, swiftly. His nose didn't break easily, only his ribs, he told her, and his lips—his lips tended to get busted and bleed when he boxed, because they were big. He asked if she had long arms, and before she could answer, he took her hand across the table and guided it to where his bottom left rib stuck out because it had been broken clean through, leaving it to float unattached in his body.

The waiter came and poured their wine. When he was gone, she took the German Boxer's hand and guided it to the same rib on her body, which jutted out at the same angle, and had been that way for as long as she could remember. "How is that possible?" he asked in surprise. "You must have broken yours too." But as far as she knew, she had never broken any ribs. The ribs, it seemed to her, went all the way back to the beginning, and were trying to say something amid their generational confusion about what it was to be a man and what it was to be a woman, and if these things could be said to be equal, or different but equal, or no.

3
—

Her bed, which was queen-size, was too small for the German Boxer, and so he had to curl up in it like a child. The light from a Himalayan salt lamp cast his torso in a warm, pinkish hue. They spoke about: his growing up on a farm near the North

Sea and how, when his family went to other people's houses for dinner, they always brought flowers picked from the fields, how this had instilled in him a sense that all flowers should look as if they had been stolen; the books they liked; whether it was strange to be a German man in bed with a Jewish woman whose grandparents were Holocaust survivors; her sister; his brother; the fact that she never wanted to get married again; the fact that nowadays it was often older women with much younger men, men who wanted to have children that the women, like her, had already had; the problem with monogamy; the problems without monogamy; his belief that boxing was not about violence but about discipline, physical discipline and the discipline of facing his fears.

Then it was four in the morning, and he said he had to go home. She told him he could sleep there. But he couldn't, he said, sitting up and pulling on his jeans. He couldn't fall asleep with someone else in the bed. When she expressed surprise, his face darkened. "No one likes it," he said, as if a referendum had been held and the results decisive. When his wife left him for another man, she'd told him that it was because the other man held her as they fell asleep. Of course there had been other reasons for her dissatisfaction, too. When she finally admitted that she was in love with someone else and was going to leave the German Boxer, she did it by phone, and during the conversation he took notes so that he wouldn't forget anything. These he took down on the endpapers of *Ghosts by Daylight*, a memoir by a journalist on her twenty years of reporting from war zones. And at the top of the list, underlined twice: the fact that he had been unable to hold his wife through the night.

It wasn't that he didn't wish he could sleep next to someone, he told her now. He simply couldn't find any peace that way. He remained alert, on edge, and so it could take him hours to fall asleep, a problem that was exacerbated by the fact that he knew that if he didn't get enough sleep, he was likely to get a migraine. He had been getting migraines since he was thirteen. They arrived with an aura that blacked out parts of his vision, and when they came the only thing he could do was curl up in a fetal position until they passed. Though it was impossible to say exactly what caused them, he was certain that lack of sleep was a factor, and so sleep had become of paramount importance. Only when he was alone did he feel at peace, and then he fell asleep moments after his head touched the pillow. It had been like that always, he told her. The last time he could remember sleeping well with someone next to him was when he was five, and had asked his mother to sit by the bed and hold his hand. But he still remembered the serenity of that, the goodness. And yet, whenever the German Boxer spoke of the unhappiness his inability had caused his wife and other women since her, his tone became frustrated and resentful: Why couldn't they understand that it was bad for him to share a bed? That it caused him to suffer?

On the only night they ever slept together in a bed—they were in the middle of a forest, he had no choice—he asked her if she minded if he said the Lord's Prayer. He had just flipped her over, pinned her arm hard against her back, and leaned his two hundred pounds into her. Now they were lying peacefully, her back against his stomach, his long arms around her. "*Vater unser im Himmel, geheiligt werde dein Name,*" he whispered. "*Dein Reich komme; dein Wille geschehe, wie im Himmel so auf Erden.*"

Freedom

I

That same summer—the summer her boys were thirteen and ten, and she was sleeping and not sleeping with the German Boxer—she'd been driving with her friend Rafi back from the moshav where he'd grown up, outside of Tel Aviv. The name of the moshav was Freedom, though it sounded better in Hebrew, less remarkable, but all the same that was the place he was born and had grown up, and as they approached on a dusty road that wound through the fields of orange trees, their children shouting in the back seat, he told her that when he'd at last begun to see a therapist at the age of forty-two, he'd asked aloud, almost to himself, in the way that one can ask unanswerable questions aloud in the presence of such people, "What do I want? What is it that I really want?" To which the therapist had answered, "What you've always wanted: Freedom."

It was Saturday, and they'd left Tel Aviv early that morning. Rafi had texted her when she woke to ask what she was doing with the kids, and to suggest that they go somewhere all together. Where? she'd written back. To the fields of my childhood, he replied. Their children, all boys, got along well enough that they usually wandered off to kick a ball or climb something, leaving her and Rafi alone to talk. Rafi was a dancer, had been one since the age of three, when he'd begun in his mother's dance studio. Everything always began and ended for him with the body, whereas she had spent many long years in her mind (or so it felt to her), and had only fully emerged into her body after she'd borne one child and then another, after she'd fulfilled the commands of her biology, and having done with it, at last took up true residence in her body, and started to dance at the age of thirty-five. Sometimes they talked about this, and sometimes they talked about their relationships, or the things they still wanted from life. The boys ran wildly around the playground where Rafi had lost his virginity. He'd had sex everywhere around there, he told her—in that building once abandoned, behind that shed, up on that dry, grassy hill.

Afterward they all went to his childhood house, and the boys filled their pockets with red lychees from the tree and got bitten by nasty ants in the grass, and then they drove to the neighboring Arab village for lunch and got chastised by the owner of the hummus place for giving their dog water from a bowl that humans ate out of. A plastic takeout box was brought with the water, which the dog didn't want anyway.

Now they were on the highway driving home, and she was saying to Rafi that all week people had been telling her the most astonishing stories. She was not aware of having asked for these intimate and staggering stories about their lives, but maybe in her way she had been; maybe she had the look of someone who was trying to work something out, something at once vast and fleeting, which could never be approached head-on but only anecdotally.

The sea was going by turquoise in the passenger window. The kids were laughing or complaining.

"I told you the one about the chicken under the car in Lebanon, didn't I?" Rafi asked. No, he hadn't, she said; she would have remembered if he had.

Rafi might have been a dancer, but from the ages of eighteen until twenty-three he'd been in the Sayeret Golani, an elite special forces unit known for the physical extremes demanded of its soldiers. To become a man in his country was to become a soldier—being a soldier was the passage you had to go through, whether you liked it or not, on the way to becoming a man, though no one could say exactly when along that passage it happened that you stopped being a boy. The first time you fired your gun at a moving target? The first time you saw the enemy as an animal? Or the first time you treated him like one?

Like every other eighteen-year-old, Rafi had no choice but to enlist. But it had not been required of him to go through the grueling selection process to be chosen for the special forces, or the year of masochistic training that followed, nor had it been required, after completing three years of necessary service, to sign on for another two years as an officer. Yet it had always been Rafi's understanding with himself that he would serve in the special forces, in a unit that would push him to the furthest limits of his physical and mental capacity. That he would become an animal, but a pure animal that operates on instinct alone, like the flying tiger that was the symbol of the Sayeret Golani, and which its commandos received during the induction ceremony in the form of a small metal pin.

"There would be a field of thorns," Rafi told her, "and you'd have to cross it. And to do so, your mind simply has to refuse to consider the pain. To think only about getting across, to make the pain irrelevant." Or there was Hunger Week, during which the recruits were not allowed to eat or sleep for seven days. Each evening, the officers would make a barbeque next to the starving recruits. They would grill steaks, lay out a feast, and then they would say to the recruits, "Come, why don't you eat with us?" And if someone gave in to his hunger and ate, that was the end: just like that, he'd fallen, and that same day he was sent back to the regular infantry. Once the officers gave out chocolate balls. "Just a small treat," they said, "we'll all eat them together," and on the count of three the soldiers put them in their mouths and bit down on what turned out to be balls of goat shit.

Of course he had been ready to die for his country, Rafi told her. To believe that one was willing to die for one's country was the bare minimum required to even enter into the selection process, though along the way there were many boys or men who discovered that they were too afraid to die or to suffer, who couldn't dissolve their fear so that it seeped out like an odor from the pores of their skin, and the moment this was detected, they were immediately disqualified. It was not until later, after Rafi was discharged from the army and fell in love, that he came to see the grotesqueness and absurdity of dying for one's country, of dying and also being willing to kill.

In the back seat, their boys became quiet: the oldest one, the only one with a phone, had taken it out, and the others were leaning in to see.

2
———

It had happened when he was an officer, during the years that Israel had occupied southern Lebanon. His unit was given the assignment to kill the Hezbollah leader in the region. Intelligence knew that every single day at 6:30 a.m. sharp, the Hezbollah chief left the house and got into his car, and their instructions were to rig the engine with a bomb. There were fifteen men in Rafi's unit, and they were carried over the border by helicopter and dropped at a mountain hideout. At 10:00 p.m., they set out crawling down the mountain and through the fields. For four hours they dragged themselves along on their stomachs until finally they arrived at the village. There was a UN convoy there, and the peacemakers were up laughing and drinking, because the UN people are always happy, Rafi said, for them it's just one long party. The unit slid past the UN tent on their stomachs and surrounded the house of the Hezbollah leader. As the officer of his unit, Rafi was positioned near to the front door, and it was then, lying on his stomach with his gun trained on it while the explosion specialist disappeared under the car, that he noticed the pairs of children's shoes. Three or four pairs lined up at the entrance, little rubber sandals just like he and his brothers used to wear on the moshav, when they wore shoes at all. No one had mentioned any children. Though why would they have? Children had no value in the calculus of military operations or wars. And in all of his nearly five years in the army, no one had ever told him anything beyond what he needed to know, and he hadn't asked. About civilians, the question had only ever been: Should you encounter one in your mission, what will you do? Of which the only three options were: kidnap, kill, or let go, where no answer was right or good. And yet the fact that Rafi had not known about the children and now was lying ten meters from their sandals disturbed him. At that moment he felt a tap on his shoulder and, lifting his eye from the crosshairs of his gun, he saw the face of the explosion specialist, painted dark green like his. The specialist gave him the thumbs-up: the bomb was in place, rigged to go off the moment the Hezbollah chief touched his foot to the gas pedal. Rafi signaled to his men to retreat, and for four hours they crawled back on their stomachs to the mountain hideout, where they collapsed in exhaustion.

By then it was close to the hour that the Hezbollah chief left his house every day and got into his car. An unmanned aircraft flew overhead and provided grainy footage of what was happening on the ground, and at 6:20 the unit gathered around the display monitor and waited. There on the screen was the house they had left four hours before, dark and still. First it was 6:28, then 6:30, then 6:35, and nothing; 6:45, 7:00, 7:15, and still only that haunting stillness. "What the fuck?" someone said more than once, possibly many times. Intelligence had established that each day without fail, at 6:30 a.m. sharp, the Hezbollah chief stepped out of his house and got into his car. So what was going on? Seven thirty arrived, and still nothing. Rafi radioed to the general of the Northern Command. *"Boxer to Kodkod North, over. What's happening? Kodkod North to Boxer"*— because Boxer was always the radio name of Rafi's position, the officer of the antiterror unit—*"Kodkod North to Boxer, stand by, over."* Then, just after 8:00, the door of the house opened, and the whole family stepped out.

Rafi, who was holding the monitor, felt himself grow cold. In the grainy picture, the father, the mother, and three children approached the car, opened the doors, and disappeared inside. The bomb was rigged such that turning the key in the ignition and engaging the engine activated it, but detonation occurred only at the first millimeter of movement on the gas pedal. At the first millimeter of movement, the car and all of its passengers would be blown to pieces. The doors of the car closed, and now there passed a moment of stillness before the key was turned and the engine came alive. "*We have ignition,*" came the confirmation over the radio.

"The seconds that followed, as I remember them now, were the longest of my life," Rafi said. "I sat watching and waiting, in a state of complete and total horror. One second, two seconds, five. And then after ten seconds, the driver's door opened, and the Hezbollah chief got out, bent over to look under the car, and pulled out a chicken."

It must have been a family chicken, beloved enough that someone in the car would have asked about its whereabouts before they pulled away. *Where is*—whatever her name was—*look, she's not there with the others!* Or, *I just saw so-and-so run under the car, she hates it when we leave, she always does this.* Or whatever one of the kids piled into the back seat said the moment before their father applied the first touch of pressure to the gas, which would have exploded them all in an instant.

"Out came the chicken," Rafi said, "and then the guy ducks down again for a second look, straightens up, and orders everyone out of the car. All the doors flew open, the kids tumbled out along with the wife, and everyone went back into the house. Around me, many of my soldiers were furious—all of that for nothing, the mission had failed, our superiors were pissed off as hell."

And him? she asked. How did he feel?

"The thing is," he said, "that I can't remember. And the more time passes, the more I feel I need to know what it seems I will never know: whether I was relieved, whether I understood at that moment that that chicken had saved my life, too, or whether I was no longer even an animal, and had become a machine."

3

It was the late afternoon now, and they were driving away from Freedom, a fact that wasn't lost on either Rafi or her. She'd had boyfriends one after another before marrying, and then after a decade of marriage she'd gotten divorced, and after that she'd been with a younger man for a long time, until now at last, for the first time in twenty years, she wasn't attached to any man at all. It was a lack that had first produced in her a sense of terror that went so far back that she couldn't identify its source. At the start of what had become a nightmarish period, she had met a friend for lunch who'd said to her, "There is no woman, however loved, who isn't terrified of abandonment," and for a very long time she'd tried to work out what that meant. Was it only because the friend was much older, shaped by a time in which women had little or no access to the avenues that might lead to self-sufficiency and independence, that she believed that? When she herself thought about it, there was very little left that a man could give her that she really needed, aside from sex, which was easy enough to find. After six months of panic attacks, unremitting insomnia, and depression, the fear of being alone, without the life support of a man, had at last receded and been replaced with a feeling of quiet euphoria.

As for Rafi, a year earlier he and his wife had decided to open their relationship of twenty-three years. They had a good and loving marriage, the heat between them had remained, and still they had arrived at the decision together, with the desire for growth and new discoveries. At first Rafi was unsure if he would ever want another woman. He thought he might be like his father, for whom his mother had remained the main force in his life, and to whom his father had remained entirely dedicated. And then, while at a residency abroad, Rafi slept with a much younger dancer from Korea, with whom he thought he was in love, until he met another from Thailand who blew his mind. When he returned home, the Thai woman broke things off from Bangkok, and after some weeks of pain, there was a very young French woman, then two or three Israelis. Meanwhile, during that time, his wife went to the beach with their children, and while they played in the waves with the dog, she met and fell in love with a man fifteen years younger than her.

Rafi and his wife had not made any rules before they started. To make rules about freedom had seemed antithetical; either that, or they had been too impatient to hold the dreary, diplomatic conference that would have been necessary to establish such rules. But very quickly it had become clear that the absence of rules led to enormous pain, and though love can be mutual and shared, pain only ever happens in a place of radical aloneness.

During the tumultuous period that followed, both Rafi and his wife, Dana, had often called her to talk. She had heard the story from both sides, or the two different stories, which as the weeks passed came to resemble one another less. She'd had to be careful not to share with Rafi what Dana confided in her, and not to share with Dana what Rafi confided in her, which became more difficult and exhausting as their stories diverged, and the pain and anger on both sides became greater.

Dana remained with the younger man for five months. The days and nights when she would return to their apartment after making love to him, or during which she would endlessly check her phone for his texts, were nearly unbearable for Rafi. He would sit smoking a joint on the terrace, surrounded by the brown, shriveled potted plants that hadn't survived the brilliance of the Israeli sun, and sometimes he listened to the sea, and sometimes he realized that he was talking aloud to himself. What did the young boyfriend give her that he didn't? He, who all his life had been a dancer, had always found that everything began and ended with the body, but Dana was an actress and a playwright, and she had always moved as fluently and swiftly in language as she had through space, and he couldn't always reach her there, in the realm of words. Could the boyfriend? Rafi had experienced enough pleasure in new bodies to know how exciting it was; that much he didn't have to imagine. And yet of course he couldn't help but imagine it all, regardless. He drove himself crazy imagining it, and when at last he couldn't take any more pain, he broke down and asked Dana to end the relationship with the boyfriend, but two days later he changed his mind again, having absorbed the fact that if she ended it because he'd asked her to, that might also be the end of the experiment, and he was no longer who he had been before it began. In other words, he no longer wondered whether he was a man for whom the main force in his life was the one woman he was married to. He was finding things out about himself, his sense of himself was expanding, and he didn't want to lose his new freedom, however painful it was to live next to his wife while she enjoyed hers.

But it was too late. In the meantime, Dana, who had taken his pain to heart and did not want to destroy their marriage or their family, had told the boyfriend that they had to end things. And he came to agree: the situation was too much for the boyfriend, too. He wanted to have children, and though he was in love with Dana, he wished to find a woman he could make a life with, one his own age who wasn't already married to someone else. Dana was heartbroken, and even more so when she found out, soon afterward, that he had begun to date a yoga teacher. She watched his online activity on WhatsApp so closely that she could tell when he was doing something outside of his normal schedule. If she texted him, she waited to see how long it took for there to be two blue checks, and if the checks stayed gray, she was miserable, and if the checks became blue, even if he didn't reply, she knew that he still thought about her. Dana missed everything about him, but most of all, she became obsessed with the sex that she'd had with him.

During this period, Dana spoke to her so often about the size of the boyfriend's anatomy that at a certain point, after many weeks and months, she finally had to tell Dana that she could no longer hear about it. Though she understood that it had become a sort of stand-in for many other things that Dana wanted or needed, all the same she found it hard to relate to Dana's obsession, since, in her experience, an enormous penis wasn't always the most comfortable sort to have inside you, especially when one had a fine penis at home already, one that had been enjoyed for twenty-three years, belonging to a man with whom one had gone through so much and still loved. To this, Dana replied that what had looked like happiness had, in the light of fresh experience, turned out not to be happiness after all, but something she'd told herself was happiness because she hadn't known better. But we very rarely can know better, she pointed out to Dana, we simply know something different, since our memories of the past must always adjust to keep our stories coherent. A point with which Dana agreed, but was helpless to employ.

It was around the time that a ban had been placed on the discussion of the penis that, during one of the many terrible fights that Rafi and Dana had, Dana had let something about it slip. She had said it, and once she had, there was no way to take it back. After that, according to Dana, the fights became more violent, and for the first time in their long relationship, the illusion of equality began to break down. Money, which Rafi earned and Dana did not, moved from being something that simply made it possible for them to live to being a source of power, since now Rafi lost no opportunity to remind her that she was dependent on him, that he was the one working a job all day while she was at home trying to write her play. In time, Dana came to feel that the experiment of opening their relationship had only brought pain and confusion, and that whatever growing they had done had only brought misery.

On the other hand, during the many conversations she had with Rafi during that time, he never mentioned anatomy, violence, or money. What he said was that for as long as he could remember in his relationship with Dana, he had been the one who gave more, who gave most willingly and easily, and that he had grown tired of it. That what he wanted was for the exchange between them to be more equal. And yet while he spoke of wanting an equality of giving and receiving, he never gave up on speaking about wanting freedom, though the first concerned how one was treated and valued by another inside a system of relationship that involved compromises and limitations, and the other concerned the destruction or transcendence of that system, of going beyond it to that no-man's-land where one stood utterly undefended, with nothing that one has promised and nothing that has been promised to one, but with a bright, clear view that goes on and on, all the way to the horizon.

Childhood

My boys are in the back seat, exhausted by the heat and the daylong sun, leaning their heads back and staring with glassy eyes at the passing sea, and either they are driving away from freedom, or toward it. After the difficult months of my undoing— months during which they watched over me with worried eyes, wanting to know how I'd slept, how I was feeling, not wanting to leave me, wanting to know whether my struggle would ever pass—they have been restored to their carefree state: midsummer, joyous, watched over.

My store of knowledge about them seems to me the closest I've ever come to possessing something infinite, and only a small part of it can find a foothold in language. And that's part of what is asked of us, isn't it? To be a witness, to be able to re-count our children's stories from the very beginning? Exactly when and where they were conceived, how the older favored the right side of the womb and showed little interest in the left and punched against my belly skin from the inside with a knee or fist, how the younger came into the world with a furrowed, philosophical look, a slight skepticism almost, but a willingness to be convinced, and a downy fur on his shoulders that later fell out. I've told them the stories of their births many times, but at some point something shifted, they began to insist on making me the hero of these tales rather than them. Now what they want to hear is how hard I needed to work to push them out, how I refused any pain medication because I wanted to be able to stand and walk and writhe however necessary to help them through the birth passage. They want to hear, again, how great the pain was which I had prevailed over—can I describe it? To what could it be compared? What they like, it seems to me, is to hear what an act of terrible strength it took to push them into the world, and that I, their mother, was capable of it. Or maybe what they want is to celebrate, again, the old and fading order of things, where they are not called on to protect, but are them-selves watched over and protected.

Enormous at birth, both are now so slender that their rib cages are visible under their skin when they lift their shirts over their heads. I know everything about what is visible of their bone structure beneath the skin, and about the skin itself, the precise location of each beauty mark and when it arrived, and the scars and what caused them; I know in what direction the hair on their heads grows, and the way they smell at night and in the morning, and all the many faces they went through before the ones they each wear now. Naturally, I do. When the older one worries that he is too thin and weak, I tell him how my brother had been built the same way when he was young, until—without warning, like a storm come so suddenly that someone, somewhere, must have prayed for it—a change came over him. That the thinness is in their genes, the sticks for arms and narrow waist and ribs poking out, all of it written into their bodies like an ancient story, but that sooner or later the time will come when this smallness and thinness will be overwritten, subsumed by mass, and the boys they are now will disappear, buried inside the men they will become.

Your brother? he asks, trying to imagine it. My brother who he once, but only once, saw, in a moment of fury he failed to contain, push me across the room and threaten me with a fist.

The small one is still too young to long to fall in love. He is surrounded by love, and that is still enough for him. The older one has already begun to long for it, but his body hasn't yet caught up with him. About this, he can still joke with me. For now, desire and the workings of the body are still subjects for humor, but as the months pass, something has begun to loom behind it, larger and larger. He is waiting for the changes he sees overtaking his friends and worries they will never come to him, that he will never desire the way the others do.

It's like a switch, friends who have boys tell me: one day it goes on, and after that things are never the same, the door closes on one side and opens to another, and that's that. Another friend, a man, says that he had been a quiet reader all through childhood, and then between one month and the next he began to throw chairs. This worries the older one, too: the possibility that he will no longer be who he has always been, that he will lose something of his sensitivity, so valued by everyone who loves him, that he will become capable of violence. When I go to kiss him good night, he curls his body into mine and in a nervous voice tells me that he wants to remain a child, that he doesn't want anything to change. But already he is no longer a child. He is standing out on a bank between the shore and a sea that goes on and on, and the water, as they say, is rising.

Acknowledgments

Grateful acknowledgment is due to the following publications, in which these stories first appeared:

"Future Emergencies," originally published in *Esquire*, November 1, 2002.

"Future Emergencies," selected for *Best American Short Stories*, edited by Katrina Kenison and Walter Mosley (New York: Houghton Mifflin, 2003).

"In the Garden," originally published as "An Arrangement of Light" by Byliner, August 2012.

"I Am Asleep but My Heart Is Awake," originally published in the *New Republic*, December 30, 2013.

"Zusya on the Roof," originally published in the *New Yorker*, February 4, 2013.

"Seeing Ershadi," originally published in the *New Yorker*, March 5, 2018.

"Seeing Ershadi," selected for *Best American Short Stories*, edited by Anthony Doerr and Heidi Pitlor (New York: Houghton Mifflin Harcourt, 2019).

"Switzerland," originally published in the *New Yorker*, September 2020.

"To Be a Man," originally published in the *Atlantic*, October 1, 2020.

About the Author

NICOLE KRAUSS is the author of the novels *Forest Dark*, *Great House*, *The History of Love*, and *Man Walks Into a Room*. Her work has appeared in the *New Yorker*, the *Atlantic*, *Harper's Magazine*, *Esquire*, and *The Best American Short Stories*, and her books have been translated into more than thirty-five languages. She is currently the inaugural writer in residence at Columbia University's Mind Brain Behavior Institute. She lives in Brooklyn, New York.